C000099374

M

by Pravin Wilkins

‖SAMUEL FRENCH‖

FOR PRODUCTION INQUIRIES

UNITED STATES AND CANADA
info@concordtheatricals.com
1-866-979-0447

UNITED KINGDOM AND EUROPE
licensing@concordtheatricals.co.uk
020-7054-7298

Each title is subject to availability from Concord Theatricals Corp., depending upon country of performance. Please be aware that *MORENO* may not be licensed by Concord Theatricals Corp. in your territory. Professional and amateur producers should contact the nearest Concord Theatricals Corp. office or licensing partner to verify availability.

MORENO was first performed at Theatre503, London, on 1 March 2022. The cast was as follows:

LUIS MORENO .... Sebastián Capitán Viveros
EZEKIEL WILLIAMS ....Joseph Black
CRE'VON GARCON ....Hayden McLean
DANNY LOMBARDO .... Matt Whitchurch

The creative team was as follows:

DIRECTOR .... Nancy Medina
MOVEMENT DIRECTOR .... Ingrid Mackinnon
DESIGNER .... Aldo Vazquez
LIGHTING DESIGNER .... Laura Howard
SOUND DESIGNER .... Duramaney Kamara
CASTING DIRECTOR .... Isabella Odoffin
FIGHT DIRECTOR .... Kev McCurdy
ASSISTANT DIRECTOR .... Tian Brown-Sampson
COSTUME SUPERVISOR ....Malena Arcucci
VOICE AND DIALECT COACH .... Esi Acquaah-Harrison
FOOTBALL COACH .... Oscar Russell
DRAMATHERAPIST ....Samantha Adams
PRODUCTION MANAGER ....Tabitha Piggott
STAGE MANAGER .... Rhea Jacques
PLACEMENT ASSISTANT STAGE MANAGER ....Friða Frosta
PRODUCER .... Ceri Lothian
ASSISTANT PRODUCER ....Myles Sinclair
PUBLIC RELATIONS .... Nancy Poole

CAST

Sebastián Capitán Viveros - LUIS MORENO

Sebastián Capitán Viveros was born in Mexico City and moved to the United States at a young age with his family before settling in Geneva, Switzerland. He trained at Drama Centre London.

Film credits include: *The 355, Spider-Man: Far From Home.*

TV credits include: *The Man Who Fell to Earth* (CBS/Showtime); *Halo* (Showtime); *Cobra* (Sky TV); *Our Girl* (BBC).

Theatre credits include: *Sweat* (Donmar Warehouse and Gielgud Theatre).

Joseph Black - EZEKIEL WILLIAMS

After ten productions with the National Youth Theatre, Joseph went on to train at Bristol Old Vic.

Theatre Credits Include: *The Coloured Valentino* (Arcola Theatre); *Sessions* (UK Tour and Soho Theatre); *Othello* (TNT Theatre/American Drama Group); *Romeo & Juliet* (Orange Tree); *A Streetcar Named Desire* (Rapture Theatre); *A Winter's Tale* (Cheek By Jowl); *The Hobbit* (Duke's Theatre, Lancaster; UK Theatre Award - Best Show for Children and Young People, Northern Soul - Best Theatre Production); *The Dutchmen, Twelfth Night, Much Ado About Nothing* (GB Theatre); *Jungle Book* (Greenwich Theatre); *Beauty & The Beast* (Salisbury Theatre).

He is also credited as the Fight Director of *Rabbits* by Sadie Smith, and *Eternity* by Asaro, and fight captain in most of the shows mentioned above.

Hayden McLean - CRE'VON GARCON

Hayden McLean is a promising young actor who trained at The Brit School. Since graduating, he has had the opportunity to work with some of British Theatre's most established names.

Theatre credits include: Yasha in Michael Boyd's *The Cherry Orchard* (Bristol Old Vic); debbie tucker green's critically acclaimed *ear for eye* (Royal Court Theatre and BBC/BFI Film); *Timbuktu* (Ovalhouse); *Ages* (Old Vic Theatre).

Matt Whitchurch - DANNY LOMBARDO

Matt graduated from RADA in 2014 and since then has worked extensively in Television and Theatre.

Theatre credits include: *Pine, Labyrinth* (Hampstead Theatre); *The Herbal Bed* (ETT Touring); *Spiderfly, Milk and Gall* (Theatre503).

TV credits include: *Call The Midwife, The Outcast* (BBC); *The Sex Pistols VS. Bill Grundy* (Sky TV).

CREATIVE TEAM

Pravin Wilkins – WRITER

Pravin Wilkins is a playwright, poet, and fiction writer based in Pittsburgh, Pennsylvania whose works typically deal with race and class struggle – and the many intersections between. He began writing plays during his time at the University of California, San Diego, as an undergraduate student of political science and literature; he continued his journey as a playwright by travelling to Pittsburgh in 2018 to pursue a graduate degree at Carnegie Mellon University. During the past few years, his work has been recognized by the UC San Diego Department of Theatre & Dance (whose faculty members honoured him at graduation with the Eric Bowling Award for his site-specific protest piece, *#takebackgraffitihall*) and the Eugene O'Neill Theater Center (which named *Moreno* as a 2020 finalist for the National Playwrights' Conference). In May 2020, Pravin received his MFA in Dramatic Writing from Carnegie Mellon's School of Drama. He was then selected as a Fall 2020 Writer-in-Residence at City Books in Pittsburgh; his works *Bars* (Four Walls Theater) and *Throw Away the Weaker Part* (dramatic question theatre) have been performed in digital spaces for live audiences. *Moreno* (Theatre503) is his first full production.

Nancy Medina – DIRECTOR

Nancy hails from Brooklyn, New York. She is based in Bristol and is co-Artistic Director of the Bristol School of Acting.

Credits include: *Trouble in Mind* (National Theatre); *Pigeon English* (Tobacco Factory Theatres) *The Laramie Project* (Bristol Old Vic); *Two Trains Running* (Royal & Derngate/English Touring Theatre); *Strange Fruit* (Bush Theatre); *The Half God of Rainfall* (Kiln Theatre/Birmingham Rep/Fuel); *Collective Rage: A Play in 5 Betties* (Royal Welsh College of Music and Drama); *When They Go Low* (NT Connections/Sherman Theatre); *Curried Goat and Fish Fingers* (Bristol Old Vic); *Yellowman* (Young Vic); *Romeo and Juliet, As You Like It* (GB Theatre); *Dogtag* (Theatre West); *Dutchman, Strawberry and Chocolate* (Tobacco Factory Theatres); *Persistence of Memory* (Rondo Theatre).

Nancy is one of three recipients of the 2020/2021 National Theatre Sir Peter Hall Bursary. She received Sir Peter Hall RTST award for *Two Trains Running*, the Genesis Future Director's Award in 2017 for *Yellowman*, and the Emerging Director Prize in 2014 for *Strawberry and Chocolate*.

Ingrid Mackinnon – MOVEMENT DIRECTOR

Ingrid Mackinnon is a London based movement director and choreographer.

Movement direction credits include: *Red Riding Hood* (Theatre Royal Stratford East); *Antigone* (Mercury Theatre); *Romeo and Juliet* (Regents Park); *Liminal – Le Gateau Chocolat* (Kings Head Theatre); *Liar Heretic Thief* (Lyric); *Reimagining Cacophony* (Almeida); *First Encounters: The Merchant Of Venice, Kingdom Come* (RSC); *Josephine* (Theatre Royal

Bath); *Typical* (Soho Theatre); *#WeAreArrested* (Arcola and RSC); *The Border* (Theatre Centre); *Fantastic Mr. Fox* (as Associate Movement Director, Nuffield Southampton and National/International tour); *Hamlet, #DR@CULA!* (RCSSD); *Bonnie & Clyde* (UWL: London College Of Music).

Other credits include: Intimacy support for *Carousel* (Regents Park).

Winner of Best Choreographer at the Black British Theatre Awards 2021 for her work on *Romeo & Juliet* (Regents Park).

Ingrid holds an MA in Movement: Directing & Teaching from Royal Central School of Speech and Drama.

Aldo Vazquez – DESIGNER

Aldo is a Mexican set and costume designer based in the UK. He trained at Bristol Old Vic Theatre School with an MA in Theatre Design in 2016, and holds a BA in Visual Arts from the UNAM/ ENAP, México City.

He has worked both in México and the UK collaborating with international directors and actors from Argentina, Canada, China, México, USA, UK and Switzerland.

In the UK he has worked designing graduating shows for Bristol Old Vic Theatre School and Bristol School of Acting.

In México he has been part of three of the annual Festival Internacional Teatro Universitario and also designed for the Swiss-Mexico Dramafest festival.

He has collaborated with directors like: Enrique Singer, Teatro Ojo, Angélica Rogel, Paula Zelaya, Emiliano Dionisi, He Hao, Francine Alepin and Mathieu Bertolet. And UK directors: Nancy Medina, Tom Morris, Donnacadh O'Briain and Aaron Parsons.

Laura Howard – LIGHTING DESIGNER

Laura is a lighting designer based in London and originally from Croydon. She graduated from the LAMDA Production and Technical Arts course in 2020 and was a recipient of the William and Katherine Longman Charitable Trust Scholarship.

Assistant Lighting Designer credits include: *Amadigi* (English Touring Opera) and *Constellations* (Donmar/West End).

Lighting Designer credits include: *SPLINTERED* (Soho Theatre); *Cells out* (Camden People's Theatre); *We Never Get Off At Sloane Square* (Drayton Arms); *SHUGA FIXX vs The Illuminati* (Relish Theatre); *curious* (Soho Theatre); *The Moors, Three Sisters, I Hate it Here, Sparks, Nine Night, The Laramie Project* (LAMDA).

Duramaney Kamara – SOUND DESIGNER

Duramaney is a London-based composer for stage and screen.

Theatre credits include: *House of Ife* (Bush Theatre); *Anansi The Spider* (Unicorn Theatre & Hyde Park Open Air Theatre); *Collections* (Tara Theatre); *The Death of a Black Man* (Hampstead Theatre); *Boy* (LAMDA); *Monologue Collections* (Tara Arts).

Isabella Odoffin – CASTING DIRECTOR

Theatre casting credits include: *The Collaboration, Klippies, In a Word* (Young Vic); *Small Island, All of Us, Manor, Three Sisters* and *Master Harold...and the boys* (National Theatre); *J'Ouvert* (Harold Pinter); *Antigone: The Burial at Thebes* (Lyric Hammersmith); *After the End, Extinct, The Sun, the Moon and the Stars* and *Sucker Punch* (Theatre Royal Stratford East).

TV and film credits include: *ear for eye, Boxing Day, I Used to be Famous, Girl* and *Blue Story*. As casting associate: *Mary Queen of Scots, The Favourite* and *Denial*.

Kev McCurdy – FIGHT DIRECTOR

Theatre credits include: *Typical, The Big I Am, Anthony & Cleopatra, Macbeth, The Great Wave, Home, Eyam, Othello, West Side Story, A Streetcar Named Desire, Frankenstein, Miss Saigon, Les Misérables, Phantom Of The Opera, Hamlet, The Wild Duck, Glory, Only Fools and Horses, The Whip, Holy Shit, White Noise, Pass Over, The Wives of Willseden, All About Eve, Hela, Tina The Musical, Wuthering Heights, Drifter's Girl, The Beauty Queen of Leenane, The Long Song.*

TV and film credits include: *Eastenders, Doctor Who, Keeping Faith, Hidden / Craith, Yr Amgueddfa, Bregus, Hetty Feather, Hollyoaks, The A-List* Season 2, *Canaries, John Carter of Mars, Season Of The Witch, Carmilla, The Lady Of Heaven, Protein.*

Music video credits include: Formation: "A Friend", Circles: "I See Monstas", Louis Mattrs' "War With Heaven"

Directing credits include: *The Saliva Milkshake; The Glass Menagerie, My Friend The Walrus, Middle Of The Road, Making Of A Motherer.*

Tian Brown-Sampson – ASSISTANT DIRECTOR

Tian is a British-Caribbean theatre director, producer, movement director and choreographer. Her focus lays mainly within Black, South Asian and East and South East Asian (ESEA) theatre work, new writing and promoting diversity, representation and accessibility on and off stage and in positions of power and leadership.

Directing credits include: *For Her* 还装什么男子汉 (Chinese Arts Now Festival); *Different Book Covers* (Tamasha); *Lost Laowais* (VAULT Festival); *Like Yesterday* (Young Vic); *Sentenced to Silence* (Camden Fringe); *Jollof Court* (Bunker Theatre); *Embalmers* and *The Lost Boys* (Theatre503).

Assistant Directing credits include: *Gin Craze!* (Royal and Derngate, Northampton); *Ivan and the Dogs* (Young Vic); *Does My Bomb Look Big in This?* (Soho Theatre, Tara Arts); *Under the Umbrella* (Belgrade Theatre, Tara Arts); and *Forgotten* 遗忘 (Arcola Theatre).

Movement credits include: *Two Billion Beats* (Orange Tree Theatre); *Heard* (Camden People's Theatre); and *Spring Awakening the Musical* (SOAS).

Malena Arcucci – COSTUME SUPERVISOR

Born and raised in Buenos Aires, Argentina, Malena Arcucci is a performance maker currently based in London. She uses devised and

physical theatre techniques, in combination with her background and interest in costume making and sculpture to explore new forms of storytelling. She currently works as a producer and theatre designer, and is co-artistic director of MarianaMalena Theatre Company.

Design credits include: *Friday Night Love Poem* (Zoo Venues Edinburgh); *Point of No Return, La Llorona* (Dance City Newcastle); *The Two of Us* (Theatre Deli); *Playing Latinx* (Camden's People's Theatre) and various productions in Buenos Aires, Argentina.

Associate Designer credits include: *Chiaroscuro* (Bush Theatre); *Thebes Land* (Arcola Theatre); *Tamburlaine* (Arcola Theatre); and *Dear Elizabeth* (The Gate).

Costume Supervisor and Maker credits include: *The Phantom of the Opera* (Her Majesty's Theatre); *Raya* (Hampstead Theatre); *Roundelay* (Southwark Playhouse); and *Milk and Gall* (Theatre503).

Esi Acquaah-Harrison – VOICE AND DIALECT COACH
Esi is a voice, accents and dialects coach whose work includes: *The High Table* and *Lava* (Bush Theatre, London); *Punk Rock* (Theatre Royal Stratford East); *Sex Education* series 3 for Netflix; *Beneatha's Place* and *Start* (Mountview); *Desert Boy* (LAMDA); *Pigeon English* (Bristol School of Acting); *Stop Kiss* (RADA).

Her other experiences include an exciting ten-year world tour (2010-2019 inclusive) with Cirque du Soleil's *Totem*, in which she was the lead female singer and original cast member. This was preceded by a two-year stint as Rafiki in Disney's *The Lion King* at Disneyland Resort, Paris. Session singing includes work with the likes of Luther Vandross, classical singer Jessye Norman, Michael Ball, Mariah Carey and Sir Tom Jones. She was a member of the UK's London Community Gospel Choir for several years. Esi still enjoys performing as a singer as opportunities come up, and tutors voice at RADA.

Oscar Russell – FOOTBALL COACH
Oscar is a brand strategist and graphic designer based in North London, originally from Bedfordshire. He has played four seasons of American Football with some of the best teams in the country, and has a number of theatre credits including playing the lead in an NSDF selected adaptation of *Woyzeck*.
This is his first credit as a sports consultant on a theatre production.

Samantha Adams – DRAMATHERAPIST
Sam is an HCPC registered freelance Dramatherapist Consultant, visiting lecturer, and early academic researcher. She was a performer for nearly three decades before re-training as a Dramatherapist. Her academic research interests include performance, ritual theatre, and restorative theatre practice, alongside generational trauma in relation to institutionalism, racism, and colonialism. Sam teaches the Therapeutic Stories Unit at the University of Roehampton on the Dramatherapy MA, where she also trained. She also contributes annually to the Applied Theatre MA at the Royal Central School of Speech and Drama teaching

the Pedagogy of Storytelling. Sam has led and facilitated the Health & Wellbeing Course to members at Clean Break Theatre Company since 2017 and has a small Therapy & Supervision private practice. Most recently Sam was in-house Dramatherapist for cast and crew of the National Theatre's *Trouble in Mind* written by Alice Childress and directed by Nancy Medina, and is currently undertaking Wellbeing Consultancy at the Old Vic. Sam has been an Executive Member of the British Association of Dramatherapists since 2018.

Tabitha Piggott – PRODUCTION MANAGER
Tabitha trained at LAMDA as a Leverhulme Arts Scholar, and is currently a production manager on the eStage development programme.
Theatre credits include: *Red Pitch, Overflow* (Bush Theatre); *The 4th Country* (Plain Heroines/Park Theatre); *Old Bridge* (Papatango/Bush Theatre); *The Dancing Master* (Buxton Opera House); *Baby What Blessings* (Old Red Lion); *Walk Swiftly and With Purpose* (Theatre503, Edinburgh Fringe).

Rhea Jacques – STAGE MANAGER
Rhea has worked in technical theatre and stage management since graduating from Rose Bruford in 2017. Her most recent role was ASM for the production of *While The Sun Shines* (Orange Tree Theatre). Prior to this in May 2019 she was Production Technician at the Orange Tree Theatre. In 2018 she was the Resident Technician at Greenwich Theatre, and Interim Technical Instructor at Rose Bruford College. Whilst at Greenwich, she was involved in house productions such as *The Jungle Book* (Milton Keynes Theatre), *Here, Robinson Crusoe Pantomime*, and returned in 2020 for *Sleeping Beauty Pantomime*. Rhea also assists with building and carpentry.
Orange Tree credits include: *Rice, Romeo & Juliet Up Close, Little Baby Jesus, Amsterdam, Directors Festival 2019, The Tempest* and *While the Sun Shines.*
Other credits: *Family Tree* (Greenwich and Docklands International Festival); *Exit The King* (Theatro Technis); *Lion In The Streets* (Stratford Circus); *Blood Bloody Andrew Jackson* (Stephan F. Austin University).

Fríða Frosta – PLACEMENT ASSISTANT STAGE MANAGER
Fríða is a third year stage management student at The Royal Central School of Speech and Drama. After working as a stage hand on musicals in The Reykjavík City Theatre for a couple of years, she moved to London to pursue her dream in theatre and live events. She has a particular passion for DSM-ing and show calling, her most recent credit being DSM on *Aladdin* for Polka Dot Pantomimes.

Theatre503 is at the forefront of identifying and nurturing new voices at the very start of their careers and launching them into the industry. They stage more early career playwrights than any other theatre in the world – with over 120 writers premiered each year from festivals of short pieces to full length productions, resulting in employment for over 1,000 freelance artists through their year-round programme.

Theatre503 provides a diverse pipeline of talent resulting in modern classics like **The Mountaintop** by Katori Hall and **Rotterdam** by Jon Brittain – both Olivier Award winners – to future classics like Yasmin Joseph's **J'Ouvert**, winner of the 2020 James Tait Black Prize and transferred to the West End/BBC Arts and **Wolfie** by Ross Willis, winner of the 2020 Writers Guild Award for Best New Play. Writers who began their creative life at Theatre503 are now writing for the likes of *The Crown*, *Succession*, *Doctor Who*, *Killing Eve* and *Normal People* and every single major subsidised theatre in the country now boasts a new play by a writer who started at Theatre503.

THEATRE503 TEAM

Artistic Director	Lisa Spirling
Executive Director	Andrew Shepherd
Literary Manager	Steve Harper
Producer	Ceri Lothian
General Manager	Tash Berg
Carne Associate Director	Jade Lewis
Literary Associate	Lauretta Barrow
Technical Manager	Toby Smith
Administrator	Birungi Kawooya
Trainee Assistant Producers	Hadeel Elshak, Myles Sinclair
Associate Company	45North

CHARACTERS

LUIS MORENO – Twenty-six-year-old Chicano NFL running back. Short, lean, cut. Cocky and materialistic in a "new money" sort of way. Media darling. Has a good heart, buried under more than a few layers of self-absorption.

EZEKIEL WILLIAMS – Thirty-three-year-old Black NFL linebacker. Tall and muscular – he's a big dude. No-nonsense. Self-educated and politically knowledgeable.

CRE'VON GARCON – Twenty-three-year-old Haitian-American cornerback. A lanky motherfucker. Street smart; quick-witted. The kind of guy who would get in a fight, lose, and still walk away talking shit. Extremely empathetic beneath this exterior.

DANNY LOMBARDO – Thirty-two-year-old white quarterback. Very tall; handsome by white beauty standards. Football is life: nothing before 1892 has meaning. The stadium is a temple.

SETTING

An NFL locker room, sideline, and field.

TIME

The 2016/2017 football season.

AUTHOR'S NOTES

A slash [/] indicates a point of interruption, where one character begins speaking over another.

Parentheses [( )] indicate something thought but not uttered.

Announcers/Reporters #1 & #2 are not intended to be cast. They are disembodied voices.

With deep and enduring gratitude for Colin Kaepernick and the hundreds of NFL players who knelt to acknowledge a moment of national injury, who held each other up as brothers in the face of injustice, and who persevered through hate to make a movement.

Pravin Wilkins

ACT I

Scene One

(Offseason: Mid-March.)

(Lights up on a pro football locker room. There are four lockers, three of which have gear in them: helmets sitting; jerseys hanging. There's a "Williams" jersey in one locker, a "Garcon" jersey in a second locker, a "Lombardo" jersey in a third, and a conspicuous lack of a jersey in the last one.)

(Enter **LUIS MORENO,** *swaggering in. He carries a large athletic bag and a speaker, which plays a hip-hop song about making a ton of money (something like "I Get Money" by 50 Cent*).)*

*(***LUIS*** *is getting into the music as he begins to remove football gear (i.e. shoulder pads, helmet, cleats, etc. – everything but his jersey) from his bag and place it in his locker. Eventually, he breaks out into dance and starts to make it rain, showering the stage with cash.)*

---

* A licence to produce *Moreno* does not include a performance license for any third-party or copyrighted music. Licensees should create an original composition or use music in the public domain. For further information, please see the Music and Third Party Materials Use Note on page iii.

(*Enter* **EZEKIEL WILLIAMS** *and* **CRE'VON GARCON**.)

CRE'VON. Awww shiiiiiiit what's this? Is this THE mothafuckin Luis Moreno in my locker room right now? Is this for real?

LUIS. Ay what up you that kid outta Tulane, yeah? I've seen some film of you up there with them 6-foot-5 Julio Joneses, batting that shit down. What's your secret?

(**LUIS** *daps up* **CRE'VON**; **EZEKIEL** *regards the mess.*)

CRE'VON. My secret ain't no secret – every corner from the dawn of time knows this: it's ALL about getting in they heads! Just gotta heckle em 'til you see what really gets under their skin, then keep shootin that their way. Eventually they snap. Lose focus. Make mistakes.

LUIS. Huh. That's some savage shit ese.

CRE'VON. And you know I seen you out there breakin ankles! Ain't you had the fastest forty of all time or some crazy shit?

LUIS. Well, I don' like to brag but...shit wait, yes I do and yes I did!

CRE'VON. Dayum Zeke we finna lock down the league wit this nigga!

(**EZEKIEL** *turns off the music.*)

EZEKIEL. So this is how you wanna make an entrance? This is how you wanna introduce yourself to your new team?

CRE'VON. Shit it don't gotta be all like that /

EZEKIEL. Hey. Cre'von. I got a C and four gold stars on my jersey that say right now's a good time for you to shut the fuck up.

(A beat.)

LUIS. Damn bro, I'm just over here tryna celebrate. I didn't mean nobody no offense.

EZEKIEL. Look we're a serious team, alright? And if I'm being real with you I had some reservations about bringing you on in the / first place.

LUIS. Reservations about bringing me on? Over there acting like you cut the checks? Man who the fuck you sposed to be anyways?

EZEKIEL. I'm a twelve-year veteran of this league. Let's say my word goes far around here.

LUIS. Well, it don't quite seem like your word went far enough this time.

(A beat.)

Tell me, what "reservations" you talkin about?

CRE'VON. Gentlemen come on, we don't gotta do this right now.

EZEKIEL. My reservations are that you're a hotshot who's not bringing the right mentality to this team. Pick that shit up.

LUIS. Excuse me?

EZEKIEL. Whatever *this* is, we don't do it in this locker room.

LUIS. You didn't think I was just gonna leave all that lying around forever...

EZEKIEL. I wanna see you pick it up.

> *(A beat. **LUIS** begins to collect the money from the floor. After a couple seconds, **EZEKIEL** exits.)*

LUIS. There, aight? You hap – wait, where'd that mothafucka go?

CRE'VON. He ain't usually like that, I think he's just a lil bitter is all.

LUIS. Fuck he got to be bitter about?

CRE'VON. Well...it's basically an open secret round here. Him and some of the other older guys, Coach approached em. Asked em to take a cut so we could bring you on.

LUIS. Oh I see now; so he's pissed this money's in my hands and not his.

CRE'VON. Yeah maybe somethin like that. He's also... dealin with some other shit...but anyways I don't think we got the chance for a proper introduction. My name's Cre'von, but my niggas call me Creole.

LUIS. So that mean Black people call you Creole, or everybody?

CRE'VON. Hah! Everybody.

LUIS. And why they call you that?

CRE'VON. Cuz I'm Creole, nigga.

    (A beat.)

What, you ain't never heard of no Creoles?

LUIS. It's like...an ethnicity?

CRE'VON. Ethnicity, race, fuck if I know. We just Haitians from Louisiana. But I grew up in St. Louis with my dad, not as many of us out there. You could say ya boi stood out a lil bit.

LUIS. Huh. Then ain't it a lil weird to just call you Creole? That'd be like if people called me "Chicano."

CRE'VON. You're overthinkin it dawg. I ain't about that PC college campus shit. That's what my niggas back in The Lou call me and it ain't never felt weird.

(A beat.)

And what's that word you said?

LUIS. What word?

CRE'VON. Chickano?

LUIS. Oh, *Chicano*. It means you're Mexican but you grew up in America.

CRE'VON. Well look at that, brotha, we teachin each other shit already. Anyway, I'm boutta dip outta here. I got me a fine ass lil date.

LUIS. Ay keep an eye out for 49ers though.

CRE'VON. 49ers? You mean 69ers? Cuz they the freaky hoes I'm lookin for!

LUIS. Nah nah, 49ers. Cuz it's the gold rush and we California baby.

*(**CRE'VON** laughs.)*

CRE'VON. You're funny, man. We gon' get along just fine. Just fine.

*(**CRE'VON** exits. **LUIS** puts his money in a clip.)*

LUIS. *(Mockingly.)* "Pick this shit up."

(A beat.)

*(**LUIS** stands and shuffles his feet as in a football drill: he does some jukes, spin moves. He's in some pain: he sits and rubs his right knee. He crosses himself and puts a finger to God.)*

LUIS. You gon' look after me this time, right? You gon' have me running just like before?

*(Enter **DANNY LOMBARDO**, looking like he just got back from vacation.)*

DANNY. Marino! They told me you were moving your gear in today and I just *had* to drop in.

LUIS. Danny, it's a pleasure.

DANNY. Marino Marino Ma-Louis fucking Marino. God damn. Welcome aboard.

> (**DANNY** *extends his hand: they shake.*)

So, I'm excited that you're here, but I'm also a business-oriented man.

LUIS. Oh you know I am too. I got big business.

DANNY. Do you now?

LUIS. I got business that go beyond football. I mean, I know you watched that Super Bowl, a few years back. I was on the field so of course at the time I didn't know it happened like this, but my mama was watching at home and she told me later, "Mijo, after you got the first touchdown they cut to the Nike commercial and it was you again!"

> (**LUIS** *laughs.*)

So yeah. I be all business all day, 25/8 mothafucka.

DANNY. Well, I didn't exactly mean that. I meant *business.*

> (**DANNY** *gestures toward the locker room.*)

And so, I've got a question I'd like to ask you.

LUIS. Yeah what's that, Danny?

DANNY. Well. I've seen you on the field. I've seen you do your little Cuba-Gooding-"show-me-the-money" dance when you get in the endzone. I've seen you dressed up like Deion Sanders in those post-game interviews. And yes, I saw your Nike ad during that Super Bowl. So I've got a certain picture of who you are. But I want to ask you myself. What is it that makes you tick?

LUIS. That makes me tick?

DANNY. Yeah, what makes you tick, what keeps you going, what gets you outta bed in the morning?

LUIS. That's hard to say, Danny. What'd you say if I asked you the same question?

DANNY. Hey don't play coy with me. I asked first.

LUIS. I dunno man, it's kind of a big question.

DANNY. Okay let's try something smaller. Why football?

LUIS. Why football?

DANNY. Yeah, of all the sports out there.

LUIS. I didn't wanna be cliché and be that Mexican kid who plays soccer.

*(***DANNY*** laughs.)*

DANNY. Well this isn't going anywhere. How about I just tell you what makes *me* tick. Then you can think about it and get back to me.

LUIS. Okay.

DANNY. One word and one word only. Winning. W-I-N-N-I-N-G. And I spell it out because...the tense is important.

LUIS. Well I can dig that ese.

(A beat.)

DANNY. You know how many QBs had a better passer rating than me in the last five years? Zero. You know how many QBs get paid more than me? Nine. And God knows it ain't because I'm not worth it. Nope. It's 'cause for me – I can't speak for you, but for *me* – money comes second to Super Bowls. I can't say that being in an ad in a game I lost would make me feel too great. Because money comes second to the Hall of Fame. To greatness.

LUIS. Well that's admirable, Danny. That's real admirable.

DANNY. And...how best to say this. I mean, I guess what I'm saying is if a guy were to come onto this team asking for a lot of money, a LOT of money, I wouldn't necessarily question his motives, but I would expect that person to help us win games.

LUIS. Well, any guy a front office pays top dollar for should be doing that.

DANNY. I'd also expect him to have the kind of hustler mentality to be able to...get over an injury.

(A beat.)

ANYWAYS, nice talk Marino. Looking forward to getting out there for camp.

LUIS. Yeah, yeah. Lookin forward to it...

*(**DANNY** goes to exit; before he does, **LUIS** speaks up.)*

Hey. You know what, I'm not playing that "new-guy-keeps-his-head-down" shit. I get paid a lotta money cuz I earn a lotta money. And while we're talking bout that, let's talk about how you still got the highest salary of anyone on the team. So I don't need no lectures about putting the team, putting wins above money. The two come hand in hand with me, aight? I get paid; we win games. Mathe-fuckin-matics.

(A beat.)

And don't you be questioning whether I still got it. My knee is fuckin stronger than before, if anything. I spent a whole god damn year getting this shit right again. It ain't no question whether I still got it, it's a question if anybody else can claim they even in the conversation bout who's the best running back in the league.

DANNY. Marino, I think you're taking all of this a bit personally /

LUIS. It's Moreno.

DANNY. Mareno. Sorry.

LUIS. Mo. Reno.

> (**DANNY** *doesn't try again.*)

Say it.

DANNY. Look, I didn't mean to offend you. Just know, expectations are high.

LUIS. I'm a diamond baby. I come into form under pressure.

DANNY. Hah! Alright then Diamonds. I'll catch you on the field. But don't be getting side-tracked. There's a lot of distractions in this world that can keep you from what's important.

> (*They shake hands.* **DANNY** *exits.*)

> (*A beat.* **LUIS** *finally removes his jersey from his gym bag. He hangs it up in the locker.*)

> (*Lights out. Sounds of a football practice play over the speakers (the quarterback calls an audible, the ball is hiked, feet hit the ground rapidly, players on the sideline shout "BALL BALL BALL!" to indicate to defenders the ball is in the air, players make contact, sounds of celebration etc.).*)

Scene Two

(Training Camp: Mid-July.)

(Lights up: We are on the field for a practice. **LUIS**, **EZEKIEL**, **CRE'VON**, *and* **DANNY** *are all onstage. They each run drills according to their position (maybe this is realistic; maybe abstract).)*

(**LUIS** *does a drill with* **EZEKIEL** *where he tries to evade him (maybe an angle drill. This is where two players face one another, standing about ten yards apart. To one player's right – and the other's left – are cones set up at ~three-yard intervals. The cones should be equidistant from each player. On some signal, the ball-carrier – i.e.* **LUIS** *– jogs down the line of cones, then cuts and starts a sprint as he decides which cones to run between. The defender – i.e.* **EZEKIEL** *– tracks the ball carrier and wraps them up if they catch them).* **EZEKIEL** *is successful in catching* **LUIS** *more often than not.)*

(**CRE'VON** *does a defensive-back drill with* **DANNY** *acting as quarterback. (This could be a back-pedaling drill where* **DANNY** *holds a football and stands still. As* **CRE'VON** *back-pedals,* **DANNY** *moves the ball to one side or the other:* **CRE'VON** *responds by shifting out of the back-pedal and jogging in the same direction indicated by* **DANNY**. *It's a three-step drill:* **CRE'VON** *starts back-pedaling,* **DANNY** *puts the ball to one side of his body and* **CRE'VON** *reacts, then* **DANNY** *brings the ball to the other side and* **CRE'VON** *reacts again by snapping his head around to the*

other side and tracking the ball as **DANNY**
throws it). **CRE'VON** *doesn't catch it every
time, but he does get his hands on the ball
every time.)*

*(During/between the drills, the players heckle
one another.)*

EZEKIEL. Come on now, Moreno. You think you're quick
but you givin it away with them big eyes.

LUIS. Ay you keep talking that good shit Imma have you
on your big ass.

EZEKIEL. You had a month and I haven't seen you do
nothin like that yet.

LUIS. Yeah that's just cuz it's easier to run right around
your clomping ass legs.

(A beat.)

CRE'VON. I smell blood Danny! I'm a fuckin shark and I
smell blood! It's time to get out the water you surfer-
lookin mothafucka!

DANNY. If you're a shark you got no teeth yet, rookie!
More like Kevin Hart in a baby shark costume!

CRE'VON. Ay this my second year homie I'm a veteran!

DANNY. "Ay ThIs My SeCoNd YeAr HoMiE i'M a
VeTeRaN!"

*(A beat. All continue running their drills.
Then: a whistle.)*

*(***LUIS***, ***EZEKIEL***, ***CRE'VON***, and ***DANNY*** take a
water break, conglomerating around a table
with athletic water bottles. They're out of
breath, except for ***DANNY***.)*

We aren't fucking ready.

CRE'VON. Nigga what? I been ready since summer began, for real. Get my ass out on that field with a crowd to see it.

LUIS. Yeah Danny, why you say we ain't ready? I'm ready as fuck to step out there and BOP! Give some mothafuckas the stiff arm on my way to anotha check.

>   (**DANNY** *reaches out to shove* **LUIS,** *but* **LUIS** *evades him.*)

WOOP! Spin move bitch I'm over here now.

DANNY. Everybody's out here acting like wins are going to be wrapped and ready for us like fucking iPhones on Christmas.

CRE'VON. Okay maybe where you from, y'all got iPhones for Christmas / but...

EZEKIEL. Danny's right. Just cuz we won the division last year doesn't mean it'll fall in our laps.

CRE'VON. But this time around, we got this speedy lil Mexican nigga! Wait, wait. This speedy lil *Chicano* nigga. My bad.

LUIS. I mean Mexican's fine too...

DANNY. Yeah yeah. Diamonds is fast, when he decides he's not gonna jog.

LUIS. Fool what? I don't wanna hear none of that shit from you. All you gotta do is stand like a statue in the backfield while we sprinting.

DANNY. I just do *my* job. My job doesn't literally have "running" in the fucking name.

LUIS. Man fuck you Danny!

EZEKIEL. Hey! What the fuck is this, the *Real Housewives of Atlanta*? We don't point fingers on this team. We take responsibility for ourselves and we push each other to be better.

LUIS. Thank you.

EZEKIEL. That being said, Moreno: you might be used to getting some kind of special treatment cuz you're in Nike ads and shit. But that asshole is a team captain and if he says you're slacking then you gotta pick it up. And I'm not saying anything, but you didn't get past me more than once today.

LUIS. Oh I see how it is, finger-pointing is reserved for the mothafuckas with badges. How American.

(LUIS flicks EZEKIEL's captain patch.)

EZEKIEL. Don't call it a fucking badge.

LUIS. You the one actin like a cop. Whatchu want me to say, huh? "Yes suh, yes suh. Sorry for defending myself, suh."

(EZEKIEL moves towards LUIS but CRE'VON steps between them.)

CRE'VON. Hey now big man. Let's take a walk. Come on.

EZEKIEL. Don't fuckin push me, Moreno.

LUIS. If the truth hurts, say ouch.

(A beat. CRE'VON sneaks a look to LUIS as he exits with EZEKIEL.)

DANNY. Damn. Not sure I've ever seen him so mad.

LUIS. I'm not sure I ever seen his ass not mad.

DANNY. You do realize "cop" is possibly the worst thing you could call him.

LUIS. I don't need a white guy from Santa Barbara to tell me cops ain't popular.

DANNY. Nah, you don't get it Diamonds. His parents were Black Panthers.

LUIS. So fuckin what?

DANNY. Look, I don't even know why I'm telling you this. None of this shit is my problem.

LUIS. Naw, naw. Go on. What's it to me who his parents are?

DANNY. Were.

LUIS. Whatever. Were.

DANNY. I REALLY don't think you're picking up what I'm putting down. They're dead. And his mom passed a couple days ago.

LUIS. Oh…shit. I didn't know that… So you're saying I should feel sorry for him.

DANNY. Well…that's not really my business.

> *(A beat.)*

But what you do on the field? That is my business. And I see you grabbing that knee when we're on the sidelines. I see past this façade you've got up. I see that you're struggling. And all I'm saying is, you better not be spoiled goods.

LUIS. I should kick the shit out of you right here.

DANNY. Better use your good leg.

LUIS. You a fuckin asshole you know that?

DANNY. Hey, you think I'm the asshole? What about you? What about the game you're playing? Sign the biggest single-year contract ever at your position, then go get yourself "re-injured"? I see right through you, Diamonds. You don't care about this game. You care about your bank account. And as you love to mention, you've already got enough celebrity: why should you care about finishing the season?

LUIS. You know what Danny, you're fucking right about exactly one thing in all that bullshit that just came out your mouth. My fuckin bank is number one. It is! I ain't got no shame in that!

Mothafuckas like you always playin this stupid shit actin like chasin money is so bad. That's cuz you ain't never hurted for it! Money's the seed for literally EVERYTHING you possibly could want. Want some food and some clothes for yo family? MONEY. Wanna travel the world, see beautiful new places, witness different cultures or what-the-fuck-ever? MONEY. Wanna get the politicians you like in office? DINERO. The whole human world's made of money – if you ain't got it, you ain't shit. And when I say you ain't shit, I mean you lower than shit. Least shit's got some place to go.

    (A beat.)

So you better fuckin believe I care about my bank. But those commas attached to this jersey. You could say I care bout this game by extension. And you know what, I did love this game before it got me shit in the bank. But even back then, I loved it cuz it got me strong. It got me girls. It got me a lil taste of what fame was all about. So yeah, maybe it's always been about somethin else for me, but so the fuck what if I don't look at that field as some holy place? So the fuck what if it's a different thing for me? That don't mean Imma pull some stupid shit like injure my own fuckin knee. Maybe you over there witchyo thirty somethin ass thinkin bout retirement, but I got *years* left.

DANNY. Oh yeah? That was a real nice little speech there. But explain the one-year contract then. If you aren't just going for the payout, what the hell are you doing?

LUIS. This the year I prove still ain't nobody got shit on me, then I get signed four years at sixty mil and I'm a happy fuckin man.

    (A beat.)

DANNY. Hold on, are you serious right now? So you're not tanking…you're betting your career? On this season? Coming off an ACL / and a…

LUIS. Yeah, that's exactly what I'm fuckin doin. So maybe you can change your attitude bout me and gimme some god damn respect.

DANNY. Yes. Yes. Absolutely. I'm a piece of shit. I take back everything I said. But…wow. You really are a gambler, aren't you? Twenty-six ain't young for a running back. You have, what. Five, six years left, tops. You should've taken the first four-year offer you got.

LUIS. None of them was enough. I ain't playin four years for less than I'm worth. I ain't you, Danny.

> (**LUIS** *exits toward the locker room;* **DANNY** *follows.*)

> (**EZEKIEL** *and* **CRE'VON** *enter the locker room.*)

EZEKIEL. I don't get why you're always taking that man's side. His attitude is fuckin toxic.

CRE'VON. I mean yeah he always be frontin, but / like…

EZEKIEL. The man is incapable of taking criticism. He acts like a (child)… Look. I'm not gonna rant to you about this. That's not how I handle my shit. That's mine and his business. But part of it has to do / with you…

CRE'VON. Hold up…

EZEKIEL. And that part is that you're emulating him / and shit…

CRE'VON. ZEKE! Hold. The fuck. Up. For just a second my nigga.

> (*A beat.*)

First of all: what the fuck you say? Emulating? I ain't fuckin understand you, man. SECOND OF ALL: you

tryna be too many things for too many people right
now. You gotta be you for YOU real quick!

EZEKIEL. What the fuck are you talkin about?

CRE'VON. I'm just sayin like, you tryna be a leader for
everybody right now and you gotta take a minute to
just...process stuff for yourself...

EZEKIEL. Are you saying cuz my momma died that I can't
act as the fuckin captain on this team? You sayin I don't
got what it takes to do my fuckin job?

CRE'VON. Nigga I'm sayin that I see through yo lil façade
and I see that you hurtin, and I see that you needa take
a god damn minute to come to grips with whateva you
goin through. Which I god-fuckin-damn imagine is a
lot, and I sympathize, and I emulate witchyou.

(A beat.)

EZEKIEL. You mean empathize?

CRE'VON. Yeah. The fuck I say? Emulate? See that's you
fuckin me up.

EZEKIEL. So you've lost a parent?

CRE'VON. Well... My moms wasn't around when I was
growin up, but that ain't really the same. You can't lose
somethin you never had, you know? But I lost people.
So I can empathize, like. With that pain.

EZEKIEL. Can you empathize with the struggle of lettin
down your pa(rents) – your pops?

CRE'VON. Nah nigga, he had low ass expectations.

EZEKIEL. Then you wouldn't understand what I'm goin
through right now.

CRE'VON. Maybe if you use yo words, you can help me
understand.

(A beat.)

What?? I ain't tryna be a asshole right now, I'm tryna be here for you cuz you be the stoic type who lets shit boil deep down and you just needa let that shit boil over for a / second.

EZEKIEL. Her last words to me were "you can still do somethin great in this life."

CRE'VON. Wha – that don't make no sense! I mean you / you...

EZEKIEL. I ain't shit.

CRE'VON. Nigga you came from nothin and now you gettin paid to ball... You a fuckin inspiration. How it is you ain't shit?

EZEKIEL. I ain't shit compared to her. I get paid to run around and smash the shit out of people. What is that really?

CRE'VON. Whatchu mean "what is that really?" Nigga you can make any job sound dumb if you say it like that. Politicians get paid to stand and talk in front some big ass flag. Niggas in construction get paid to fuck up concrete or pour it. Writers get paid to hit keys with they scrawny-ass / fingers...

EZEKIEL. Alright I take your point, but what I do still ain't shit to a woman who helped break Assata outta prison.

CRE'VON. Assata? Who's Assata?

EZEKIEL. How you never heard of Assata Shakur? Mothafucka this is why you gotta educate yourself: you know white America ain't gonna teach you bout any Black revolutionaries who they didn't kill in the end. It ain't a good look for them so they just leave it out.

CRE'VON. Hold up, she related to Tupac?

EZEKIEL. Okay, I already know I'm not gonna get you to read a whole ass book, but at least listen to "A Song for Assata." Common? *Like Water for Chocolate*? Shit man, you can give six minutes for the culture. Long story short, Ms. Shakur fought for our rights and got put in prison for it and my momma helped break her out. Needless to say, that don't leave this room...then again, I guess it doesn't matter now.

CRE'VON. Damn nigga yo mom gangsta as fuck.

EZEKIEL. Yes...that's definitely one way to put it. Another would be to say she devoted her life to our struggle. And I always thought, you know, if I made it, if I ended up somewhere besides the corner or the cage, that'd be a testament to her. To her work as a mother, as an activist. To the work she did to move us forward.

CRE'VON. So you free now cuz she fought then. Ain't that a win?

EZEKIEL. She didn't see things like that. Naw...after I got drafted, you know what she said to me? She said "Zeke, don't do it. Don't you sign yourself away to the plantation. They're just gonna use you up and spit you out, broken. Broken of mind and body." I didn't say nothin. I knew I wasn't gonna change her mind. She always saw sports as one of the tracks the white man offers us to keep us happy, but where we ain't really gonna change shit. So I already knew how she felt. But she kept goin anyways. She wasn't gonna let the moment pass without getting her piece in. "They auction you off," she said, "then they buy you, sell you, trade you. They even got you out on a field. Cuz to them, you're field niggas. Ain't nothing changed but the money."

CRE'VON. That's crazy bruh, we ain't field niggas. We just niggas who happen to be on a field. Them owners don't control us.

EZEKIEL. But don't they?

CRE'VON. No fuckin way. They own some of our time, yeah. But that ain't no different than any job. We gotta

give em some hours and we gotta answer to em when
it's about business. Everything outside that, that's
yours.

EZEKIEL. But maybe they own us in a different way. Maybe
they own our minds. Maybe when the money keeps
coming in and the cameras keep flashing and the
whistles keep blowing, when the reporters keep asking
you the same questions again and again and again
and you give your scripted non-answers, when you
keep donating that lil something to a charity cuz it's
a good look for the league and it makes you feel a bit
saintly, just saintly enough...maybe it's like hypnosis.
They drag you along by your ego and convince you that
you're steering.

CRE'VON. I really wish I could help you figure that but my
mind ain't wrappin around what you puttin down.

EZEKIEL. Give it another five years. At that point...either
you'll know what I'm talking about or you'll be lost in
the whirlwind.

CRE'VON. Nigga you on some Langston Hughes shit right
now.

EZEKIEL. Well, least you know who he is.

CRE'VON. Yeah I'd love to meet the nigga.

(EZEKIEL *facepalms.*)

CRE'VON. I'm just fuckin witchyou! Why so serious, nigga?
Come on. We gotta get you a drink or somethin.

EZEKIEL. Nah. No blue pill for me tonight. I got shit I
needa think about.

CRE'VON. Shit, well alright then Morpheus.

Yeah I know, finally you drop a line I get. Anyways I
hear you – if that's what you gotta do that's what you
gotta do. Just keep your head on you.

*(*CRE'VON *exits.* EZEKIEL *is alone onstage.)*

(A beat. Lights out.)

Scene Three

(Pre-season Week One: Early August.)

(Lights up on the locker room: triumphant hip-hop music (something like "All I Do is Win" by DJ Khaled*) plays over speakers as **LUIS** *and* **CRE'VON** *get down to it.* **DANNY** *is primping himself up, presumably for a post-game interview.)*

DANNY. Guys, come on. It's the fucking pre-season.

CRE'VON. But nigga we mopped the floor with those mothafuckas! That shit was a slaughter!

LUIS. Man, maybe two or three of them fools got two or three fingers on me all day!

> *(***EZEKIEL*** *enters and starts changing from athletic attire into street clothes.)*

EZEKIEL. Hey can somebody turn that off real quick?

DANNY. Jesus, gladly.

> *(***DANNY*** *turns off the music.)*

CRE'VON. Ay come on man!

EZEKIEL. So who's heard about Kaep?

LUIS. Colin Kaepernick? QB on the Niners? What about him?

EZEKIEL. Folks around the league are saying that he's been sitting down during the national anthem for the last

---

* A licence to produce *Moreno* does not include a performance license for any third-party or copyrighted music. Licensees should create an original composition or use music in the public domain. For further information, please see the Music and Third Party Materials Use Note on page iii.

couple games. They're speculating if it's a political statement.

CRE'VON. Yeah nah I heard about that. Somethin tells me that nigga just misses the spotlight. Ain't nobody been sayin his name much since that Super Bowl L (loss).

EZEKIEL. Come on Creole. Why do brothers always assume the worst from each other? Is it so impossible that the man's got something important to say?

DANNY. Come on, Zeke. Creole's right: it's obviously just about relevance. He can't get it done on the field anymore so he found some other way to get people talking about him.

LUIS. Ay Danny, to be fair you'd be strugglin too if you was playin with that ugly ass squad. I mean who they even got in the backfield now that Frank's outta there?

CRE'VON. That's a good point; and who the fuck Kaep got to throw the ball to? The ghost of Jerry Rice?

(A beat.)

EZEKIEL. Danny you just assume it's about the game cuz you've never had a non-football-related thought.

DANNY. Yup. And that's why I got three rings. No small part of the reason YOU got three rings.

EZEKIEL. I'm just saying I want to hear what the man has to say.

LUIS. I don't know dawg I ain't really got the energy for all that political drama.

EZEKIEL. What do you mean you don't got the energy?

DANNY. Maybe he means he's busy doing his job. Speaking of which, I've got an interview. Nice work out there today, gentlemen.

LUIS. Ay you too D.L.!

(**DANNY** *exits.*)

CRE'VON. You and "D.L." sure tight now.

LUIS. Yeah, well now that I convinced him I ain't out here tryna pull a Sam Bradford he basically worships my ass.

EZEKIEL. That's because his world begins and ends on that field. That how you work too, Moreno?

LUIS. Nah, I ain't like him. He got obsession where I got appreciation.

CRE'VON. Yeah come on now Zeke, you know this nigga's world begins with Dom Perignon and ends with ass.

(**LUIS** *and* **CRE'VON** *laugh.*)

EZEKIEL. I'm just trying to place you is all. Cuz Danny I can understand. A white man who doesn't give a shit about anything except the one thing he's good at? Yeah, I can see that. But when you ain't white...you can't lose yourself all the way in passion like that. There's always something else happening. Something else to keep track of. To watch out for. Shit, if you ain't white, money and fame ain't freedom. It's just insulation.

CRE'VON. Swear this nigga been talkin in riddles the past month now.

EZEKIEL. What I'm saying is, why you acting like you got the privilege to not give a fuck about what's goin on outside your little personal bubble?

LUIS. Maybe I got enough problems without piling on every fuckin thing that happens in the news.

EZEKIEL. Yeah but I'm not over here talking about the persecution of Muslims in Myanmar; I'm talking about a man who wears the same cleats and pads we do.

CRE'VON. Oh and that nigga got some funny ass socks.

EZEKIEL. Jesus fucking Christ, Creole. I'm trying to have a serious conversation here.

CRE'VON. Ay I'm just sayin them socks he got with the cops lookin like pigs be fuckin comedy.

EZEKIEL. Cops looking like pigs...

LUIS. Look I can't keep track of every fool in the / league.

EZEKIEL. I know what he's doing... He's protesting police violence.

> *(A beat.)*

> *(**EZEKIEL** pulls out his phone as he hurries off stage.)*

LUIS. Is he aight?

CRE'VON. I mean...

LUIS. Like I know me and him go at it, but I feel for that man, losin his moms. I can't fuckin even start to imagine losing mi madre. Shit, I ain't even wanna think about that. She the one person I could never stand to see nobody fuck with. Far as Zeke...maybe it's the same way. Poor mothafucka's all over the place.

CRE'VON. Nigga walks with a weight I ain't never gon understand.

LUIS. Fool take him to the club or somethin.

CRE'VON. He ain't like us though. He don't forget his problems when you get a drink in him. He think up whole new problems.

LUIS. Huh. Well you think that shit he was talkin about, that shit about Kaep, you think that's gonna be somethin?

CRE'VON. I mean if I was guessin myself, I'd say nah. But Zeke do seem to think it's a big deal, and that nigga on some Harvard shit compared to my black ass.

LUIS. Well...one way or the other, ain't really on my radar.

(Lights out. A beat.)

(Projection (or audio) of the famous August 28, 2016 interview in which Kaepernick* finally speaks out on the issues over which he has been protesting.) (Note: In the event that permission is obtained, Kaepernick's answers, to a minimum of two reporters' questions, should be included here).)

(Projection/audio fades out as next scene begins.)

---

* A licence to produce *Moreno* does not include a licence to publicly display any third-party or copyrighted images or audio recordings. Licensees must acquire rights for any copyrighted images or audio recordings or create their own. For further information, please see the Music and Third Party Materials Use Note on page iii.

Scene Four

(Pre-season Week Three: August 28.)

(Lights up on **EZEKIEL***, who sits in the locker room watching Kaepernick's interview on his phone.)*

*(***DANNY*** enters and sits next to* **EZEKIEL***.)*

DANNY. Looks like the publicity stunt is paying off.

*(***EZEKIEL*** pauses the video.)*

EZEKIEL. Have you listened – sat down and actually *listened* – to a single word he's said?

DANNY. Why should I reward him with my attention?

EZEKIEL. We're not talking about a misbehaving toddler right now we're talking about a grown ass man who's speaking up about grown ass issues.

DANNY. Come on, Zeke. This media grandstanding bullshit is exactly the type of nonsense you've always cracked down on in this locker room. I mean, your professionalism, your focus, it's something we all count on around here. What about last year even, when Creole was skipping Monday practices / because he wanted...

EZEKIEL. That's completely different. You know I got love for Creole but sometimes he just acts like a straight-up fool...look, Danny. Isn't the fact that I of all people am taking this so seriously a sign that it's no flash in the pan? Isn't the fact that a man you've never known to fuck around is really mulling this over, isn't that a hint that this is NOT just about some...some petulant kid trying to get his way?

DANNY. You know, Zeke, I defer to you on that. Maybe he's not a sideshow. Maybe what he's doing is bigger. But if

Kaepernick wants to be a politician, why not hang up
the cleats and put on a tie?

EZEKIEL. You act like you gotta be in office to be involved
with politics.

DANNY. I'm just saying there's a time and a place for /
those conversations...

EZEKIEL. Danny, let's be real. For the conversations people
aren't having, for conversations about issues that most
people in this country don't like to think about, the time
and place never comes. Unless you make it happen.
Unless you force it. And Black people have been talking
about the police killing us for decades and nothing is
different today.

DANNY. Man...but why's it got to be mixed with football?
Why do those conversations have to happen *here*?
What, don't look at me like that – I'm serious! This
locker room, that field...they're sacred spaces. Spaces
where it's just X's and O's, routes and coverages,
touchdowns and interceptions. Glory and failure. I
mean, people got a million problems they deal with
every day. Some folks deal with racism and yeah that's
not right. And everybody's got personal problems. But
Sunday from noon 'til eleven PM is when people are
supposed to put all that aside and come together and
enjoy this beautiful game. It's supposed to be one of
those few places where we aren't constantly reminded
of the thousand shit-storms we're in.

EZEKIEL. You know Danny, when you put it like that, I'm
not gonna lie it does sound nice. Almost like a little fairy
tale. But some of us...we can't just put our problems in
a box and deal with them when it seems convenient.
Cuz they follow us. Everywhere we go, every room we
enter, every pair of eyes that locks with ours.

DANNY. Zeke...the way you're talking, it sounds like next
Sunday I'm gonna "oh say can you see" you sitting too.

(A beat.)

EZEKIEL. That was a terrible joke.

DANNY. I hope you're talking about the idea itself. We are just finally getting everything working. Creole's got that little shade-the-wideout-to-the-sideline technique perfected. Moreno's got the playbook down and is looking to be back at 100 percent. You're out there running like you're twenty-five again. This could be *our year.* I know you wanna be in that big game again. It's been, what? Six years? The last thing we need is to get bogged down by distractions.

EZEKIEL. Distractions...

DANNY. Yeah, distractions.

EZEKIEL. But what if this is the distraction, Danny? What if the yards and the touchdowns and the fumbles and the collisions, what if the rings and the accolades and the commentators spouting our praises, what if Super Bowl wins, Hall of Fame inductions, documentaries on our success...what if those are the distractions?

    (A beat. **EZEKIEL** *exits.)*

DANNY. Fuck.

    *(***CRE'VON*** *and* **LUIS** *enter, wearing gym clothes.)*

CRE'VON. ...And I was like "damn baby is yo tongue in my ass right now??"

    *(***LUIS*** *and* **CRE'VON** *crack up.)*

LUIS. No fuckin way! It feel good?

CRE'VON. Not gonna lie...

LUIS. *(Imitating the meme.)* Hah! Gaaayyy!

DANNY. Hey, can you two act like professionals please? The season starts in two fucking weeks.

    *(***DANNY*** *storms out.)*

LUIS. Oh shit, what's his problem?

(**LUIS** *and* **CRE'VON** *begin to change from athletic gear to street clothes.*)

CRE'VON. I mean it could be one of a hunnid things with that nigga, but also, well...he don't like when people make, uh, gay jokes.

LUIS. But like it's a meme... And he ain't even gay! Right?

CRE'VON. Naw. His lil brother gay though. Guess niggas used to make fun of him for it. He'd get in fights and shit tryin to defend him.

LUIS. Seriously? How I never knew that?

CRE'VON. You know that man live a pretty segmented life. He don't bring his personal shit to this room too often. Or like, at all.

LUIS. So how you knew bout that?

CRE'VON. Well...long story short, at a practice last year I was jokin around and I called one of them wideouts... well, the f word. Afterwards Danny pulled me aside and he explained all that. And you know like I said before I ain't really bout that political correctness shit, but long as I ain't hear that nigga say nigga I guess I can respect that he don't wanna hear that type of shit.

LUIS. Yeah... I'll keep that in mind. On my old team people was tossin that word around on the daily.

CRE'VON. Shit nigga, same. Danny don't stand for it though.

LUIS. Hm.

CRE'VON. What?

LUIS. Naw, it's just. I think this is straight up the only time I thought of that fool as anything but my QB. Like, as a person with a family and shit. Somebody's brother.

CRE'VON. Well to be fair, ain't often he invite you to think of him that way. And shit he a good enough QB he ain't gotta look elsewhere for definition.

LUIS. I hated his fuckin guts for the first month or two but shit at this point there ain't no other quarterback I'd rather have. Except maybe a Mexican one.

CRE'VON. Shit there even a Mexican QB in the whole league?

LUIS. Fool there's barely any Latin players in general. I'm a rare breed.

CRE'VON. Watch out nigga they gon make you the spokesperson for your race.

LUIS. Shit guey if it comes with a check then I'm your new expert!

(*CRE'VON and* LUIS *laugh. A beat.*)

(*Cre'von's phone buzzes: he takes it out and notices something unexpected.*)

CRE'VON. Oh shit...check this.

(*LUIS peers at Cre'von's phone.*)

LUIS. (*Reciting from phone.*) "This stand wasn't for me. This is because I'm seeing things happen to people that don't have a voice, people that don't have a platform to talk and have their voices heard and affect change."

This Zeke?

CRE'VON. Naw that's a quote from this video he sent.

LUIS. Oh that's Kaep, dawg! Holy shit fool that video's twenty minutes long!

CRE'VON. Oh fuck. Getchyo popcorn ready.

(*Lights out.*)

Scene Five

(Regular Season Week One: Early September.)

(Sounds of a full stadium echo through the room.)

*(Lights up on **EZEKIEL** and **CRE'VON** in the locker room. **EZEKIEL** is helping **CRE'VON** stretch/get taped up in preparation for a game.)*

*(Elsewhere (but still in the locker room), **DANNY** and **LUIS** are getting ready too.)*

DANNY. So Diamonds, I've been thinking...that play where we got you motioning out wide to make the defense show their hand...if you hear the mike call an audible, I want you to motion right back across, all the way to the other side, and just line up for a screen.

LUIS. So if it's man-to-man I'm a decoy and if it's zone I be read number one?

DANNY. Exactly.

LUIS. Got it. Got it. Shit man I'm straight feenin to get out there.

DANNY. That week one itch.

CRE'VON. You ready to get out there and bust some heads my nigga?

EZEKIEL. Always ready.

CRE'VON. You just ain't seem as hyped as usual.

EZEKIEL. Nah?

CRE'VON. You thinkin bout sittin, ain't you. Along with Kaep.

EZEKIEL. He ain't sitting anymore.

CRE'VON. Wait, he done protesting?

EZEKIEL. Nah, not exactly.

LUIS. Yo D.L. you know how Coach got me on a snap count cuz he tryna ease me back in?

DANNY. Yeah.

LUIS. Do me a favor and don't make me sit back there pass blockin when I am out there.

DANNY. If pass blocking is what the play calls for, you'll be pass blocking.

LUIS. Hey I know it sound like I'm just tryna get the ball all day, but I promise you. It's in the interests of the whole team for me to get fed.

DANNY. Oh yeah? Noted.

CRE'VON. So if he ain't done protesting, whatchu mean he ain't sittin?

EZEKIEL. Last week he took a knee instead. Apparently he talked to a friend who serves in the military, some guy named Nate Boyer. He told Kaep the whole sitting thing kinda rubbed him the wrong way and that he'd feel better about the protest if Kaep took a knee instead.

CRE'VON. Damn so that nigga Colin tryna make people happy even though they be torchin him anyways.

EZEKIEL. Just like Obama.

CRE'VON. Damn... President Obama. Why ain't they lettin the man run again? Like fuck a term limit, this the first Black President of all fuckin time.

EZEKIEL. I hear that.

LUIS. Look man, I get it if you need me pass blockin when we're goin deep. But if the play got me back there blockin when we're going for ten or less, lemme just run a quick out or something.

DANNY. You realize that backfield blocking assignments exist so I don't get fucking rocked by some blitzing linebacker.

LUIS. Come on man they ain't even really hittin QBs any more.

DANNY. I don't care about taking the hit, I care about losing yards.

LUIS. But you won't lose yards if you just flip it to me when they blitz.

DANNY. Please, just do your job.

LUIS. My job is to win games mothafucka, like you always talkin about.

DANNY. No, *our* job, as a *team*, is to win games. Your job is to execute the play.

LUIS. Except you seem to be forgetting I'm the best in the game. That means my job is to take the ball down field. They ain't payin me to pick up blitzes man, they payin me to get yards and get in the endzone. Just trust me this time, and if it ain't workin then I'll hang back and block for you.

DANNY. Jesus Christ. Okay. But the first time I get hit by someone you should've / had...

LUIS. I got it, Danny. You won't regret it.

CRE'VON. Wait so Zeke. You never really answered me. You gonna take a knee today?

EZEKIEL. Look Creole, let's keep our minds on the task at hand, which is coming out and starting off the season with a win.

CRE'VON. Aight man. Aight.

(A beat. All players should be fully suited for the game.)

> (**DANNY** *begins stomping in rhythm; other players begin stomping in unison and gathering together.*)

> (*A chant begins.*)

EZEKIEL. HARD WORK!

DANNY, LUIS & CRE'VON. DEDICATION!

EZEKIEL. HARD WORK!

DANNY, LUIS & CRE'VON. DEDICATION!

EZEKIEL. HARD WORK!

DANNY, LUIS & CRE'VON. DEDICATION!

EZEKIEL. HARD WORK!

DANNY, LUIS & CRE'VON. DEDICATION!

> (**DANNY** *moves toward the middle of the room, raising a helmet (which silences the chant), and addresses everybody.*)

DANNY. Alright gentlemen, let's get it done! Together on me together on three; ONE, TWO, THREE:

DANNY, EZEKIEL, LUIS & CRE'VON. TOGETHER!

> (*Chorus of "hell yeahs" and whooping sounds from the players.*)

> (*The players jog off stage in single-file.* **DANNY** *is in front, followed by* **LUIS**, **EZEKIEL**, *and* **CRE'VON**.)

> (*Crowd noise intensifies. Over speakers, a voice booms.*)

ANNOUNCER #1. And now, kicking off the season at home, let's welcome our team, led by three-time Super Bowl champion: Danny Lombardo!

(**DANNY** *jogs onstage: he is on the field. He is followed by* **LUIS**.)

Just behind Lombardo we have a newcomer to the team: superstar running back and former league MVP, Luis Moreno!

(**EZEKIEL** *and* **CRE'VON** *jog out.*)

And there's the defense bringing up the rear! Looks like the whole team has taken the field!

(*Now, all four players stand on the sideline.*)

(*A beat. Continued applause/stadium noise.*)

ANNOUNCER #2.   And now, ladies and gentlemen, to honor America, please stand and remove your hats for tonight's performance of the national anthem!

(*Crowd noise dies down. The mood changes. Maybe lights go up on the audience. Maybe a large American flag is unfurled. The anthem begins.*)

(**DANNY** *puts his hand over his heart.* **LUIS** *crosses himself. And then...*)

(**EZEKIEL** *takes a knee. The other three take notice.* **DANNY** *is exasperated;* **LUIS** *only glances over and looks away;* **CRE'VON** *appears to have a moment of indecision – he then places a hand on* **EZEKIEL**'s *shoulder.* **CRE'VON** *raises a fist. Lights out.*)

Scene Six

(Two spotlights, each on a podium. At one podium stands **LUIS** *wearing flashy clothes; at the other stands* **EZEKIEL** *in a suit and tie.* **LUIS** *is smiling cockily: a Cam Newton-esque smile.* **EZEKIEL** *is stoic. Neither is aware of the other's presence: think of them as being in totally separate press conferences. Throughout this section,* **REPORTERS** *will ask questions to* **LUIS** *and* **EZEKIEL**: *their voices are pre-recorded or come from offstage; each time* **REPORTER** *speaks, it is a different voice.* **REPORTER** #1 *talks to* **LUIS**; **REPORTER** #2 *talks to* **EZEKIEL**.)*

EZEKIEL. Alright I know y'all got questions.

LUIS. Wooooohhhhh!!!! It is good to be back! Okay who's first?

*(**LUIS** points out a **REPORTER** he "sees.")*

Go ahead.

REPORTER #1. Luis, we know this was a big win for you. Tell us how you managed to break 200 yards from scrimmage in your first game back after what some thought could have been a career ending injury you sustained less than a year ago.

LUIS. Ay well, you know it's been work! It's been work. I just really wanna thank this organization for believing in me and I wanna prove them right for bringin me out here. I can't do nothin from the sideline, so I knew I had to do everything in my power to get back in condition to be out on the field. And when I am on the field, shoot, 200 yards could happen any time. Let's see if we can hit 250 next week.

*(A beat. **EZEKIEL** gestures at a **REPORTER**.)*

REPORTER #2. Ezekiel, people noticed that you took a knee during the national anthem before the game today – are you joining in Colin Kaepernick's anthem protest?

EZEKIEL. Yes. Yes I am. And it's not an "anthem protest," it's a protest against *police brutality* and *systemic racism.* Colin's been pretty clear with what it's about.

(*A beat.* **LUIS** *gestures at a* **REPORTER.**)

REPORTER #1. We saw you really involved in the passing game tonight – is that something we can expect to see more of moving forward?

LUIS. Well hey I'm not tryna blow up coach's gameplan or anything.

(**LUIS** *chuckles at his own joke.*)

But y'all know I can do it all. I'm out here tryna get yards however they come. Keep it movin forward.

REPORTER #2. So what do you say to folks who are offended, who think this protest is disrespectful to the armed forces?

EZEKIEL. I say to those folks that I'm offended they can't ever have a serious conversation about racism in this country.

(*A beat.*)

I mean, it's the same sh – same stuff different decade for Black people. Don't protest this way, don't protest that way. Make it peaceful. Oh, it's peaceful now? But you're blocking roads and making people late to work. Oh, it isn't getting in anyone's way at all now? But you're disrespecting our troops. It's #AllLivesMatter all over again: this country would rather make up an issue than deal with the real issues that affect Black people every single day.

(*A beat.* **LUIS** *gestures at a* **REPORTER.**)

REPORTER #1. Do you have any comment on your teammate, Ezekiel Williams, and his decision to take a knee during the anthem today?

LUIS. Huh. You know to be honest witchyall I didn't really notice that. I did see that fool strip the ball and take it for a fifty-yard house call tho. Y'all see that?

REPORTER #2. So are you saying that you don't care if people think you're disrespecting the troops?

EZEKIEL. Are you serious? Look at that, the spin's already on before ink hits print. Does anyone wanna ask me about the issues we're protesting? Does anyone wanna ask me about what y'all can do to help our cause?

(*A long beat of silence.*)

Hm. Alright then.

(**EZEKIEL** *leaves the podium and goes to the locker room.* **LUIS** *gestures at another* **REPORTER**.)

LUIS. Yeah, you in the red.

(*Spotlights off. A beat.*)

(*In the locker room:* **EZEKIEL** *sits on the bench, watching a video on his phone. He shakes his head and puts his phone away.* **LUIS** *enters.*)

Ay big dawg, whatchu still doin around here?

(**EZEKIEL** *glances up, unimpressed.* **LUIS** *begins to change from his flashy outfit into sweats.*)

EZEKIEL. Just got caught up watching that video of your press conference.

LUIS. Oh yeah, that shit. I mean if it was up to me I'd just go from the field back home, but you know how it is.

EZEKIEL. You sure you didn't like it a bit? Seemed like you were glowin under those cameras.

LUIS. I mean, I'd be lyin if I said I didn't dig it a lil bit. Seein myself on YouTube, on the TVs at sports bars. But shit half the time I just wanna pull a Marshawn and skip out.

    (A beat.)

EZEKIEL. So is "I didn't notice" really the best you could do?

LUIS. What?

EZEKIEL. When they asked you about me – at the press conference. About me takin the knee.

LUIS. I mean, I was just bein honest, I really didn't even see it.

EZEKIEL. A person who's telling the truth usually doesn't have to say "just bein honest" every time they say it.

LUIS. Man this was my first game in almost a year; I had some tunnel-vision goin on. I didn't see nothin but that field.

EZEKIEL. Mothafucka you were standing right next to me. You can tell that shit to the press if that's how you wanna play it, but don't fuck with me. I know you saw me.

LUIS. Aight man, fine. I saw; what the fuck is it to you? I lied to those reporters cuz I'm not tryna get all up in that mess right now. Maybe you got time for that shit, but I don't. I got bigger things goin on.

EZEKIEL. Oh, you got bigger things goin on?

LUIS. Yeah Zeke, I got bigger things goin on than some dumbass wokeness fashion statement. I got a contract to play for. I'm talkin ones and zeroes and the commas in between. Cuz that's real.

EZEKIEL. You think this shit is a fashion statement to me? Mothafucka I'm out here putting my career on the line. Maybe fashion is all your diva ass, MTV *Cribs* ass knows anything about, but that ain't where the morning starts for everybody. I guess you don't know the struggle or you went and forgot where you came from. Cuz if you came up in section eight, if you came up in the hood, you'd have people you lost cuz of the shit Kaep is talkin about. You'd have people you lost and people still goin through it. So maybe you don't know bout that shit. Or maybe you just ain't see it anymore. Maybe you washed your hands of all that. After all, a house in Beverly Hills does something to a man. Next thing I know Imma turn on the news and it's gonna be you sayin "I'm not Latino, I'm Moreno."

LUIS. Aight I've fuckin heard enough. It ain't like that. I remember exactly where I came from. They called my block the barrio of busted windows... You ever heard of San Ysidro? Naw, I doubt it.

Mothafuckas like you always think you grew up in the hardest hood, like its some competition who dug their way outta more shit to get up. Well I'm not lookin for pity or to play that game. But lemme say this: I seen lots of people stick their necks out for what's right just to get their throats slit cuz of what ain't. So you can play this superhero, Atlas bullshit; Imma worry bout gettin mine, for myself. For my family.

EZEKIEL. Well, least you tacked "family" on at the end there.

LUIS. Don't you fuckin question what I do for my family! You don't know my life! I gots people livin off me, aight? I gots people countin on me to get this bread. I got family who used to have to work in dirty ass factories to make the threads you got on your fuckin back!

EZEKIEL. Good to know there's a little left over for em after you got that third Bentley. Or was it an Aston Martin?

LUIS. I'm fuckin done with you man...

EZEKIEL. Naw, naw. You ain't done with me 'til I'm done with you. And I got you pinned, Moreno. You're one of them types who be on that "God is good" shit now that everything panned out for you. God is good cuz he got you. And if he ain't got you, shit. That's just how it is, huh. Tell me that ain't how you think.

LUIS. So that's it, you got me pinned huh? Bitch, I got YOU pinned. I know you doin whatchu doin because your fuckin mama died thinkin you was a failure. Yeah. I fuckin know bout that. And now you caught up on your own hype, tryna to act like you the second coming of Jesus or somthin? Man you ain't shit.

(A beat.)

EZEKIEL. Yeah. You're right: I ain't shit.

(Another beat.)

You wanna hear me say it again? I. Ain't. Shit. And maybe what I'm doin now, maybe it does come from a place of guilt; maybe it comes from a place of shame that runs deeper than you could ever know, but this is bigger than me now! And it's not going away. This protest? This battle? It's not one where you get to abstain. It's not one where you get to sit out. Because sittin out is the same thing as choosin a side.

LUIS. And why's it matter so much to you what I do?

EZEKIEL. Cuz who am I? Who the fuck is Ezekiel Williams? It doesn't matter that I been in the league over a decade. This is the Country of New. You play a fuckin song from over four years ago, brothers tell you that shit's old. You think people wanna hear from me? I don't have what you got. I don't have cameras in my face whenever I step out. I don't have the whole sports world contemplating who Imma sign with. You got power, Moreno. You got all this power, and no will.

(**EZEKIEL** *exits.*)

(**LUIS** *gets pensive.*)

(*Lights out.*)

End of Act I

ACT II

Scene Seven

(A montage of victory. Projection of the team's record starts at 1-0, switches to 2-0, then 3-0 and so on until the record reads 7-0, at which point this sequence will end.)

*(During this sequence, all players but **EZEKIEL** take the field: they run, they juke, they catch the football, they knock it down (Note: the actions they perform should be specific to their position, so we should not see **DANNY** defending a pass, for example). Maybe they stand at podiums all dressed up, maybe they celebrate in the locker room. All the while, **EZEKIEL** is taking a knee in the middle of the stage. **CRE'VON** occasionally acknowledges him, maybe raises a fist in solidarity once or twice. **DANNY** and **LUIS** act as though he is not there.)*

*(Just before the projection reads 7-0, all players leave the stage. **LUIS** bursts onstage in full uniform, carrying the football. He runs from one side of the stage to the other, juking, twirling, leaping as he goes. Maybe he does this in slow motion. Maybe it feels like a dance. When he gets to the other side of the stage, he soaks up the glory. Crowd cheers*

over speakers. He does his famous "show-me-the-money" celebration.)

(**LUIS** *spins the football on the turf with flair: as the ball spins,* **DANNY**, **CRE'VON**, *and* **EZEKIEL** *return to the stage, rushing the field after* **LUIS***'s game-winning touchdown, dancing around the ball, maybe warming their hands over it like a campfire. They all continue celebrating until the ball stops spinning, at which point:)*

(The projection reads 7-0, the montage ends, and the players are huddled up in the locker room, teeming with energy. Stadium noise can still be heard echoing through the walls.)

EZEKIEL. Bring it in yo bring it in. On me!

DANNY, LUIS & CRE'VON. SAY WHAT?

EZEKIEL. GIVE YOU!

DANNY, LUIS & CRE'VON. MY BLOOD!

EZEKIEL. GIVE ME!

DANNY, LUIS & CRE'VON. MY DUB!

EZEKIEL. AND ANOTHER?

DANNY, LUIS & CRE'VON. And another, and another, and another, and another, and another...

(Lights out. All **PLAYERS** *exit.)*

Scene Eight

(Week 9: Mid-November.)

*(Lights up on the locker room. **LUIS** enters: he is hot. He launches his helmet at one of the lockers and wails. It sounds like he's in pain. Or maybe like he wants to fight somebody.)*

LUIS. Fuck! Fuck fuck fuck fuck fuck!

*(**LUIS** sits on the bench and breathes heavily. He is freaking out.)*

*(**DANNY** enters and rushes over to **LUIS**.)*

DANNY. Hey! Hey man what the hell is going on? Is your knee tweaked?

LUIS. It ain't my knee man, it ain't my knee.

DANNY. You hurt something else?

LUIS. Look D.L. you ain't the right person for right now.

DANNY. Diamonds you're in here sounding like you're straight up dying – I need you to tell me what's going on.

LUIS. It's my mama she. She...

DANNY. Did something happen to her?

LUIS. No, she just... Danny can you please just get Creole? Can you bring Creole in here?

DANNY. Luis / I...

LUIS. If you tryna help me right now I need you to fuckin listen to me and get Creole and send him in here! Aight? I ain't need you grillin me I need you hearin me!

DANNY. Okay, fuck. I'm going. I'm going.

(DANNY exits. LUIS is trying not to break down.)

(A beat.)

(CRE'VON enters and rushes to LUIS.)

CRE'VON. Yo yo yo yo yo. What's goin on nigga? I saw you take that call and dip out the practice. I was finna follow you but Danny said / he had it...

LUIS. I don't fuckin know what to do man, I don't know what to do.

(LUIS is about to break down.)

CRE'VON. Hey, hey. Shit man. Come here.

(CRE'VON wraps his arms around LUIS, who maybe starts to cry.)

I gotchu brotha. I gotchu. You my family and I gotchu.

(LUIS starts to calm down.)

LUIS. It was my mama on the phone, she sayin she wanna... she sayin some guys came by at night and graffitied up the walls at the taco shop she work at. Really tore up the place. She sayin she wanna leave the country cuz she ain't feel safe no more. Sayin she wanna pack right up and go.

CRE'VON. Goddamn what the tag say?

LUIS. Build the wall. Go home, illegals. They say this to people who been here, who they stole this land from.

(A beat.)

Man I told her a minute and a fuckin half ago she ain't gotta work there no more, cuz I got money now and I could get her a new crib on a damn hill somewhere and she ain't gotta work no more if she don't wanna. And that woman, she choose to stay there. She choose to keep workin. Cuz everybody knows her there, she got friends and family and... And she love makin people's days. It sound stupid but she really and truly love the look on people faces when she hand em a jamaica and some tamales just like she make for her own family. And this the thanks she gets from this worthless fuckin bullshit ass country?

CRE'VON. Ay I hear you man, I hear you. But she gots to have had people bein racist to her before. I ain't tryna be insensitive I'm just sayin... I done sprayed over a lotta tags in my day that got me heated and ain't never thought about leavin.

LUIS. She was there when those pandejos came by. That's my mama, stayin late, always making sure everything's clean as her own home for the next folks who take over for her. She saw em from the drive-thru window, dressed in all black, wearing masks. She told me she wanted to run, but she was too scared. So she hid behind the counter. She heard glass shatter; a brick flew over her head. A fuckin brick, Creole. Inches from her face.

CRE'VON. God damn.

LUIS. And on top of it all, man, these ain't just some assholes on the street. These the mothafuckas runnin shit now, runnin the fuckin country. Or at least, they're homies with the guy up top.

CRE'VON. I still can't believe that racist cantaloupe lookin bitch finna be the President...

LUIS. I don't know what to do. Creole, I just... I don't know what to do. When my mama called it low-key sound like she packin up right as we were talkin. I wish my pops was still around to...you know. Calm her down. Make her feel safe. And I can't be there either cuz all this shit...

CRE'VON. Hey. Your momma need you. You be over 1,000 yards and we only halfway through the season. Ain't nobody finna question your commitment. You gotta go see her. It's God first, then family, then football. You gotta be with her right now. Just go.

LUIS. You right, you right.

> (LUIS *removes his shoulder pads and grabs a bag from his locker and exits without changing the rest of his clothes.* CRE'VON *takes a deep breath.*)

> (*A beat.*)

> (EZEKIEL *enters.*)

EZEKIEL. Cre'von we're trying to run a 7-on-7, what the fuck you doing chillin up here?

CRE'VON. Luis goin through a bit of a crisis right now.

EZEKIEL. Always something goin on with that man...

CRE'VON. Well...this time a bit different. He really...he hurtin.

EZEKIEL. Where's he at?

CRE'VON. On his way to San Diego.

EZEKIEL. Come again?

CRE'VON. Zeke. Lemme tell you somethin. You wrong about that man. You wrong about him.

EZEKIEL. Man this ain't the time or place / for this...

CRE'VON. It's the time and it's the place cuz we both right here.

EZEKIEL. Oh is that how it works.

CRE'VON. I'm just sayin that maybe if you knew what I knew about him maybe you wouldn't write him off so easy.

EZEKIEL. Okay, you know what? I don't owe it to you to hear you out right now. I bore my soul to you thinkin you'd be discreet with the things I told you. Then when push came to shove, that asshole pulled out my momma's dying words on me like a fuckin pair of pocket aces! I shoulda kicked the shit outta him. But you know what I did instead? I bore my soul again. Hoping, hoping he would listen. Hoping he would use that fucking colossal platform he got to say he supports me speaking my mind, at the very fuckin LEAST. And what does he go and do? *Nothin.* Dodging questions like a fucking Democrat Senator being asked about Standing Rock.

CRE'VON. Standing Rock?

EZEKIEL. Forget it, man! The point is that Moreno's nothing more than an iced-out clown and you betrayed my trust. My confidence!

CRE'VON. I already told you I was sorry bout tellin him that shit! How many fuckin times can I tell you that, nigga? I was tryna get him to see things from your perspective, I didn't know it'd play out like that! I just been tryna help you and him see that you ain't so different deep down!

EZEKIEL. Hah. We ain't so different? Me and Luis Moreno ain't so different... See if I knew you was tryna pitch me your comedy routine I'd have left a minute ago.

CRE'VON. You know what, fuck it. Let's run this 7-on-7 then. If you ain't wanna talk to me like a man.

EZEKIEL. I'm thirty-three years old, lil nigga. I don't take that bait no more.

> (**EZEKIEL** *exits.* **CRE'VON** *reluctantly follows. Lights out.*)

Scene Nine

(Week Nine: Postgame.)

(Lights up on the locker room. **DANNY,** **EZEKIEL,** *and* **CRE'VON** *all enter in full gear, winded and dejected.)*

(A beat of conspicuous silence.)

DANNY. Okay, is anyone else gonna say it?

CRE'VON. *(To* **EZEKIEL.***)* Odds we get spared from havin this conversation?

EZEKIEL. Say what, Danny?

CRE'VON. Oh, zero. Dope.

DANNY. We lost because Diamonds flaked out on us.

CRE'VON. *(To* **EZEKIEL.***)* Hey, team captain. You wanna speak up on behalf of your teammate?

EZEKIEL. I'm captain of the defense. If Danny got business with Moreno, I don't see what business that is of mine.

CRE'VON. Great, well ain't that just great.

DANNY. Hey, I'm just saying. I don't understand why people are acting like it's okay that he just disappears on Thursday and then phones Coach to tell him he won't be here for the game.

CRE'VON. I mean they already probly gonna cut his pay cuz of it.

DANNY. The fuck I care whether or not he gets paid? I'm saying we lost because he wasn't out there with us. Doesn't that piss you off? We could still be undefeated. Chasing history.

CRE'VON. You realize his momma was dealin with a hate crime.

DANNY. Yeah, and he was there for a whole two days. From San Diego back here, it's a one-hour flight and a three-hour game. He could have been in and out and on his way back over there as we speak.

(**CRE'VON** *looks at* **EZEKIEL** *as if to say: "aren't you going to say something about that?"*)

CRE'VON. Huh, well look at that. I guess I'm outnumbered here. Cuz SILENCE (*Looks at* **EZEKIEL.**) is a form of choosin a side. So yeah. Shit. I guess you right Danny. I guess two days shoulda been enough time to talk his momma outta leaving the country and help his community heal. Fuck him, right?

(*A beat.*)

What happened to us not pointing fingers on this team, huh? Cuz shit, if Danny gonna start pointin fingers, maybe I'll take this finger and point it right in your fuckin face, Zeke, cuz you was out there tonight getting your ankles broke!

(**EZEKIEL** *doesn't take the bait.*)

Aight you know what, nah. I'm fuckin takin my shit...

(**CRE'VON** *gathers his things.*)

I'll see you niggas back home.

(**CRE'VON** *exits.*)

DANNY. Well. He's a bit emotional.

EZEKIEL. He's also right.

DANNY. Right about what, exactly?

EZEKIEL. Danny, sometimes the best thing you can do is step back and not say shit.

DANNY. Yeah that's all well and good except for the fact that I'm gonna be the one who gets asked about

Moreno's absence in all these post-game interviews. I'm
the one who has to explain why we couldn't get it done
without him. So I'm gonna have to say shit whether
I like it or not.

EZEKIEL. And what are you gonna say then?

　　　(A beat.)

DANNY. Well of course I'm going to back him up in front
of the reporters. But between you and me, I think he
should've been out there.

EZEKIEL. Hm. I guess you gotta take that up with him
then, huh.

DANNY. I'm just saying, you know. You're always out
there from the kickoff to the last whistle. You got a lot
of fans pissed off by joining that protest, but at least
you don't pull shit like this. At least you're there for us
when it counts. Now, 'cause of Moreno? Chances for an
undefeated season...totally fucking spoiled.

　　　(A beat.)

　　　(Lights out.)

Scene Ten

(Week 10: Early December.)

(Lights up on the locker room: a game has just ended. **DANNY** *is changing from gear into business attire.)*

*(***LUIS*** *enters and starts to hastily change from his gear into interview attire that is more professional than usual (for him).)*

DANNY. So you're with Zeke now, huh?

(A beat.)

Don't think I didn't notice you take a knee today.

LUIS. Well. I ain't doin this for him.

DANNY. Whatever man. Good stuff adjusting on that wheel route.

LUIS. I thought you'd be up my ass.

DANNY. Shit man… If you're on that field getting game-winning touchdowns, fuck it. Long as you don't EVER skip out like last week.

LUIS. Really? So you ain't mad?

DANNY. I just don't have the energy to be mad anymore. I mean, you know I'm not like those guys out there burning Zeke's jersey…like the guys who'll be burning yours tonight. I don't hate you for what you're doing. I just wanna win games, man.

*(***EZEKIEL*** *enters.)*

EZEKIEL. Yo, Moreno. All these weeks I been tryna get you to speak up and you ain't even mention to me that you were gonna take a knee today?

LUIS. I wasn't exactly planning on doin it.

EZEKIEL. You weren't planning on it? You joined a protest movement without planning on it?

LUIS. Look man, I'm just tryna get ready for this press conference.

EZEKIEL. I'm just tryna figure out what's going through your head right now.

LUIS. Aight ese you wanna know what's goin through my head? When they had that big ass flag waving over that field, when that song start and everybody standin up together, I didn't feel like I was part of that no more. Cuz I didn't hear the words to that song. All I could hear was my mama sayin to me "Mijo, they don't want us here." Now if you don't mind, I gotta figure what I'm finna say to these fuckin reporters.

> (**LUIS** *hastily exits.*)

DANNY. I thought you'd be happy, Zeke.

EZEKIEL. I don't even know what to think.

> (**CRE'VON** *enters.*)

CRE'VON. Sup gentlemen.

EZEKIEL. Creole, everybody knows you and Moreno are pretty tight. What's he up to?

> (**LUIS** *re-enters the stage but is not in the locker room. He is at a press conference.*)

CRE'VON. Look nigga I already told you I ain't gettin between you crazy mothafuckas no more. I'm keepin my head down and mindin my damn business.

> (**CRE'VON** *starts to change out of his gear.* **DANNY** *primps up his suit, then exits.*)

> (*Spotlight on* **LUIS**.)

LUIS. Aight, I know everybody gonna be askin bout me takin a knee today. Lemme tell you straight up. This racist country elected a President who thinks people like me are rapists and criminals. And now all these punk ass wannabe klansmen shitheads feel like they got power. Feel like they can crawl out from under they little rocks and harass my family just cuz we come from Mexico. Well that's bullshit. And I ain't give a FUCK how much Imma be fined for sayin it. Cuz if my own mama don't feel safe in the country she been livin in since she was a kid, I ain't feel like I'm livin in the land of the free. So that's my piece yo. No further questions.

> *(**LUIS** exits.)*

> *(Back in the locker room:* **EZEKIEL** *and* **CRE'VON** *have been watching Luis's press conference on Ezekiel's phone. He puts it away.)*

CRE'VON. Damn that nigga just went off.

EZEKIEL. He has no idea what he just did.

> *(**LUIS** enters the locker room.)*

LUIS. You fools still chillin here?

EZEKIEL. Moreno, what the hell was that?

> *(A beat.)*

CRE'VON. Aight, I'm done tryna play peacemaker with you bitches.

> *(**CRE'VON** exits.)*

LUIS. What was what, man?

EZEKIEL. Do you realize how hard people like me have been working to get the media to pay attention to the shit we're tryna talk about? Already they're making this about a million other things. Now you drop this bomb right in the middle of everything?

LUIS. I ain't the one who tagged up my mama's work and smashed up the windows.

EZEKIEL. Oh, so it's all about you, huh? You're a regular fucking Dick Cheney, you know that?

LUIS. I don't know why you be makin all these fuckin references ain't nobody gonna get.

EZEKIEL. I'm saying why aren't you capable of caring about a problem 'til it reaches out and touches you? Why is it you didn't once think to stand up for me, with me, but you got no problem using the platform folks like me built to air out your fuckin issues? This protest has been going on for months. For months, Moreno! And not once did you fix your lips to speak out about Mike or Alton or Trayvon. Not. Once. And now you wanna insert yourself right in the middle of this shit cuz that's all you ever know how to do!

LUIS. You know what, Zeke, maybe you ain't the only one with problems! Maybe you been right about a lotta things. Maybe God went and punished me for talkin shit on you bout your mama. Maybe I'm reapin what I sown. I don't know man. But what I know now is that you been right about this country. You been right. But nobody in the league standin up for people like me. Nobody thinkin to protest against this racist cabrón talkin bout building a wall to keep people like me out. So don't guilt trip me for not havin your back when you ain't never had mine neither!

EZEKIEL. You never asked! You know what, I don't think I ever heard you even talking about the problems in your community 'til they hit you dead in the face!

LUIS. Well guess what fool? They hit me! Are you fuckin happy about that? Are you?

(A beat.)

You know, I was finna walk in this room and tell you that you were RIGHT. You were right about money not being freedom for people like you and me. You were right that I got the power to do something, but I wasn't motivated to. Now I got the motivation, now I got the fire, and that ain't enough?

EZEKIEL. No! It's not! Because sometimes the fire just burns up everything!

LUIS. Ain't nothin I do ever gonna be good enough for you Zeke! You Christ complex having mothafucka!

> *(**LUIS** grabs a bag from his locker and storms off stage.)*

> *(Lights out.)*

Scene Eleven

(Week 11: The Next Day.)

*(Lights up on the locker room. **LUIS** and **CRE'VON** are resting in gym attire after a practice/workout session. They look exhausted. Not just from the exercise.)*

CRE'VON. So uh, how you been, dawg?

LUIS. Well let's see. Nobody else on the team wanna talk to me. Not even the fool I thought would have my back. Coach told me ain't no way they resigning me after that press conference – don't matter how many TDs I get. Unless I go up next week, dick between my legs, and apologize bout what I said.

CRE'VON. Damn nigga.

LUIS. And...my moms left. Put the apartment up for sale. Went back to live with my tío and his wife.

CRE'VON. Put it for sale? She owned the place?

LUIS. Yup. And she was damn proud of that too. I grew up in that apartment. There were these lil trees that grew outside, called jacarandas. Whenever they was bloomin, she would always point it out. And if there ever was more of them lil purple flowers than there were leaves on one of em, you could straight up bet what she'd say. Must have heard her say it a million times. "Mijo, mira: mas flores que hojas. That one gives more than it takes in." Then she'd go on, sayin something about how... I'm sorry – nevermind dawg. You ain't ask about none of that.

CRE'VON. I'm askin now. Come on dawg, really. I'm askin now.

LUIS. Well, she'd say we all should have a season in our lives, where we give more than we take in. She'd say you can't do that every day, but maybe some days you can.

CRE'VON. You been lucky to have a momma like that. My momma only ever taught me what I didn't wanna be. But I guess a parent always gonna teach you somethin. No helpin that.

> *(A beat.)*

LUIS. Do you think I did the wrong thing, takin the knee?

CRE'VON. Nigga please. I cover the wide receiver. I line up top of the numbers, and I jam em at the line. I'm a corner. A twenty-three-year-old, one-year-under-the-belt corner. The fuck am I supposed to say bout that shit?

LUIS. I hear you. You're a cornerback. But you also Black and you also from the hood. That shit Kaep's been talkin about, that Zeke's been talkin about? You been there. You lived that. I know you been profiled by the cops before, or at least your homies have. I don't wanna bring up no sensitive shit, but it wouldn't surprise me if you lost somebody cuz of some bitch ass cop. So when I went up in front of those reporters, when I said I'm protesting too cuz this country's fuckin over Latino people too, was that...do YOU think that took away from...

CRE'VON. I think...well, people was already tunin out from the things Kaep and Zeke been tryin to talk about. And the news this week out the league? It's definitely you. Not them. I'm tryin dawg, I'm really tryin to be here for y'all without diggin in on some side of all this, but... don't you think it's clear you stole they spotlight?

LUIS. Fuck, man. I wasn't tryin to take nothin from nobody. Something just moved within me, man. I could feel my family lookin through my eyes, my people lookin through my eyes, and seein a country that don't want em. For some of us, the only country we ever called home. Was I supposed to just shove that down? Say, well, this ain't our moment?

CRE'VON.   Look man, where I come from, ain't too many Mexican niggas. The Lou is a Black and white kinda city, know what I'm sayin? So I didn't have any Mexican or Puerto Rican or anything like that kinda friends growin up. And nigga you know I don't watch the crusty ass news. So I ain't know shit about what's goin on with Latino people in America. Shit, matter of fact, if I did watch the news I'd probly know less. But I do know you. I think in these last few months I got to know you pretty good, nigga. And what happened witchya momma? That ain't right. So if you feel like you gotta stand up for her, for your kinfolk, for yourself, who am I to say anything bout that?

LUIS.   I really appreciate you for sayin that dawg. I just feel like... Zeke don't / see it that way.

CRE'VON.   PLEASE don't drag me into the middle of y'alls' drama again. Everything I tell either of you mothafuckas just turns out to make things worse. My lips is sealed if that shit is comin up again.

LUIS.   Creole, I need you to help me, man. I can't undo what I did. I can't walk back what I said to those reporters. It ain't even that I'm afraid of lookin stupid; it's more than that. There was something I felt at that podium...something I don't think I ever felt. It was like goosebumps all through the inside of my body. No touchdown, no broken tackle, no nothin made me feel that before. I knew, I knew in that moment that I believed in what I was sayin. It wasn't no bullshit; it wasn't no show, no game. And I'm fightin that fight now. And I need Zeke on my side. And shit, he needs me. He already told me that much.

   (A beat.)

CRE'VON.   I can't tell you nothin about Zeke. But there is somethin I can tell you. But you gotta hear me out.

When I was in high school, this Vietnamese couple opened up a market a few blocks from where I was livin. I ain't really know nothin about em, but they seemed like good people. Always smilin and waving when I passed – never gave me no bad juju, you know, like them white folks who you spot givin you the up and down. And they did good business. But my dad, he hated em. Thought they oughta get off the block and go on back where they came from. When I was a kid, I never got why he felt like that. But eventually I realized...my dad hated em cuz they weren't white neither, but they got treated like they were. These two came straight from a whole ass notha country, and had it better here than folks like us ever had it. Folks who been here for generations. So there's probly a lotta niggas out there who feel they been passed over. Like their problems always the last to be dealt with, if they ever gonna get dealt with at all.

LUIS. I hear you, but Mexican people been fucked over all the same, I don't / get why...

CRE'VON. Nigga this ain't the oppression Olympics! You ain't got nothin to prove to me, aight? I'm just tellin you how some niggas feel. And when you speakin at a press conference, you ain't talkin to me. You talkin to everybody. You said the way you felt in that moment when you was speakin your truth, it didn't feel like a game? Well, if there's one thing I learned watchin Kaep deal with all this stuff, watchin Zeke deal with this stuff, it's that it's still a game homie. A whole different game. And you gotta make it yours...or they gon make a game outta you.

> *(A beat.)*

> *(Lights out.)*

Scene Twelve

(Week 11: Gameday.)

(Crowd noise and maybe some typical announcer-pregame-chatter plays over speakers.)

(Lights up on the locker room: **CRE'VON** *and* **DANNY** *are on one side of the locker room, fully suited;* **EZEKIEL** *is on the other, suiting up.)*

DANNY. Look man, I've known this QB for years. He can't throw anything right except that deep out.

CRE'VON. What if he catch me jumpin it and they do a lil chair route?

DANNY. Then believe me, it'll be an underthrow. You'll catch up to it.

*(***LUIS*** enters.)*

Diamonds! You ready to crush these guys?

LUIS. Yeah, yeah Danny. Hey, Zeke, you got a second?

*(***EZEKIEL*** turns to* **LUIS***; says nothing.)*

DANNY. Come on guys, for God's sake can we have one Sunday where we just play the damn game?

*(***LUIS*** ignores* **DANNY***. A beat.)*

*(***LUIS*** approaches* **EZEKIEL***.)*

God damn it.

*(***LUIS*** takes out some slips of paper from his pocket.)*

CRE'VON. Just leave em to it man. That ain't our business.

(CRE'VON ushers DANNY offstage.)

(LUIS puts the slips of paper in Ezekiel's locker.)

(A beat.)

EZEKIEL. What's that?

LUIS. That's five one-million-dollar checks.

(A beat.)

Sold the Phantom. Sold the Lambo. Sold the Ferrari. Sold the Aston Martin. Wrote those up last night. One for Black Lives Matter. One for the Trayvon Martin Foundation. One for Black Wall Street USA. One for 100 Black Men of America. And one for the NAACP.

(EZEKIEL scopes the checks.)

If there's better ones to donate to, I figured you could let me know. I mean, I just googled pro-Black non-profits so, you probly got a better idea of what's what.

EZEKIEL. This is... Moreno, are you serious right now?

LUIS. I'm takin a knee again today. And after the game, Imma tell them this is about more than me. Imma tell em I spoke too harsh last week, and too selfish. That it was a moment of passion I didn't know how to channel. But that was the old Moreno. The new Moreno, he stands up for himself and for his teammates. And he gon find a place for himself within this movement. He ain't takin it over. The new Moreno, he gonna pay his respect to the people who been fightin, and trust they gonna show out for him too.

(A beat. EZEKIEL and LUIS see eye to eye.)

EZEKIEL. I never thought you'd come around, Moreno. I
    thought you were just gonna keep diggin in and diggin
    in and diggin in.

    *(**LUIS** holds his hand up and out.)*

LUIS. There any chance? Any chance we can try this again,
    as brothas this time?

    *(**EZEKIEL** clasps **LUIS**'s hand.)*

    (Lights out.)

Scene Thirteen

(Weeks 12-17: A montage of victory, aesthetically similar to Scene Seven.)

(The team is 10-1; 11-1; 12-1; 13-1; 14-1; and finally, 15-1. All four players – perhaps two at a time, perhaps all at the same time, perhaps one at a time – enact football as a dance. **LUIS** *jukes;* **EZEKIEL** *takes his run step and drops into coverage;* **CRE'VON** *chases down a pass and bats down the football;* **DANNY** *scrambles out of the pocket and runs the ball downfield. In this sequence, each player should embody their position on the field, performing snippets of what the action on the field looks like without ever necessarily performing a "full" football play.)*

(At the end of the victory montage, another triumphant hip-hop song begins to play (something like "Started From the Bottom" by Drake*).)

(Late December: End of Regular Season.)

(Enter **CRE'VON** *and* **DANNY**, *wildin' out to the music. It feels like the locker room has morphed into a club.)*

CRE'VON. Zero to 100, my nigga! Slippin to double dippin, dawg! Fuck yeah!

DANNY. Three rings just ain't enough! I'm after four and then some more! I'm passing Staubach, I'm passing

---

* A licence to produce *Moreno* does not include a performance license for any third-party or copyrighted music. Licensees should create an original composition or use music in the public domain. For further information, please see the Music and Third Party Materials Use Note on page iii.

Bradshaw, I'm passing Montana and then I'm passing Tom motherfucking Brady himself!

CRE'VON. Oooooo okay, I see you throne chaser! They gon make a *Game of Thrones* meme outta you pretty quick here. The one true QB! All decked out in some fur coat, witchya slain foes on the ground in front of you!

DANNY. Hey and know what, cheers to my man Moreno, flipping the script for us down here! Last year we were still putting the pieces together, but this year? Shiiiiiiit. Where is that man? Diamonds! Heyoo, Diamonds!

>   *(A beat.)*

>   *(Where is Luis?)*

>   *(Spotlight on **LUIS** and **EZEKIEL**: They are visible to the audience, but not onstage. **CRE'VON** and **DANNY** cannot see them.)*

>   *(**LUIS** and **EZEKIEL** walk. Spotlight follows. Their faces are weary, serious. They don't look like they just got the top seed in the NFC.)*

>   *(Onstage, **CRE'VON** and **DANNY** eventually give up looking for **LUIS**. Lights and music fade.)*

LUIS. Stagnation. Huh. What a interesting word. I gotta school up so I sound like a smart white guy in interviews too.

EZEKIEL. Hey, don't play into that shit. Ain't nothing white about being educated, or well spoken. White people don't own that shit.

LUIS. Naw, I just meant / that like...

EZEKIEL. Don't hide from the meaning behind your words. You meant I sound white when I say things like stagnation. But somehow no matter how many times I say it, I'm still a man of mass melanin.

> *(A beat.* **LUIS** *doesn't know what* **EZEKIEL** *just said.)*

I'm still Black as fuck.

LUIS. Okay so you Black and you educated and there ain't nothin white about that. Point taken.

EZEKIEL. I'm just saying these little things matter.

LUIS. Fine fine, but how bout we get back to the big things. Like how we gonna get past this...stagnation.

EZEKIEL. I don't know. That's why I brought it up. It just feels like... I mean, none of the coaches are doing much to defend us. Neither are the owners – least of all our own. And fans aren't standing up for us either – at least not enough of them, since Fox News and all the fork-tongued Sean Hannitys of the world decided we hate the troops and somehow that's what this is about now. We need to do *something* to reclaim the narrative.

LUIS. Reclaim the narrative?

EZEKIEL. Yeah like, with all this bad press we're getting from these well-groomed Nazis, they got us playing defense. No matter how many times we say this protest is about Black and brown people in this country getting treated right, getting treated right by police and by the government, they shout louder than we can. These people have had the ball the whole god damn game, and we need to get our offense back on the field.

> *(A beat.)*

LUIS. What if the way to do that is to not take the field at all?

I just keep thinkin about this moment when I was talkin to Danny. When I first took a knee, I thought he'd chew me out. But naw; he told me long as I'm on that field, he don't care what I say.

EZEKIEL. Now that you mention it, he said the same thing to me.

LUIS. We can't think fans or coaches are gonna get us that bump we need. We for sure can't expect owners to do nothin. But if we do somethin drastic, if we go the extra mile, if we leave no middle ground...maybe we turn some dudes like Danny. You know, like if they really gotta make a choice to be for us or against.

EZEKIEL. Shit, man.

LUIS. What?

EZEKIEL. I swear, every generation of American civil rights fighters comes to this exact same stumbling block. How do you get the mythical conscientious white folks on your side? The problem is, you'll never get enough white people to come together to change a system that values their lives and dreams and health above all others. You know why? Because they love that about America. They love that the lie of their superiority is held aloft by a system that values and nourishes and forgives them where it bludgeons people like us. They. Love it.

LUIS. Aight yeah maybe some of em do. Shit, maybe a lot of em do. But what about dudes like Chris Long? You know, out in Philly? He's been speakin up, he been supportin us.

EZEKIEL. Still. He's the exception, not the rule.

LUIS. I don't know man. I think most white folks, it's just too easy for em to not make a decision. And I know what you always say, dawg. That that's the same as makin a decision. But I can tell you that from the other side, that decision you make every day to not change anything, it don't feel like a decision. It feel like the default. And now I understand that sometimes... it takes a big push to make people confront somethin and really deal with it. So what if we force a decision on em? I'm just sayin, if we *control the narrative,* I think a lotta people would surprise you.

EZEKIEL. So we walk off, at home, in the divisional round of the playoffs, as the Super Bowl favorite. I can see that's dramatic, but I don't see how it forces the Danny Lombardos – or shit, even the Cre'von Garcons of the league to make any kind of decision. You really think they'd just follow us?

LUIS. Without us, they lose. No question. You think Danny wants to go out there and flail around while he gets his ass handed to him, all in front the biggest audience of the whole season? It'd be an embarrassment. I say we approach him beforehand and give him the chance to walk out with us. If he comes through, bet most guys on offense follow suit. You know the clout he got in this locker room. And if a bunch of us go, it shows the whole country we gainin ground.

EZEKIEL. But you realize the power you'd be giving Danny? He could go right to Coach, or right to the press, and take the wind right out of our sails. If word gets out beforehand, a walkout would lose all its...its explosiveness.

(A beat.)

*(**LUIS** is thinking...then, a realization.)*

LUIS. I got a plan. I know what's gotta be done. Leave Danny to me. And you talk to some fools on defense. Wit that bye week, shit, we got time.

EZEKIEL. Luis, I'm not sure about this...

LUIS. Trust me, Zeke. Ain't I earned that?

(A tense beat.)

(Spotlight goes out.)

Scene Fourteen

(January: Playoff Bye Week.)

(Lights up on the locker room. There is a quietness that does not quite fit the room as we have come to know it.)

*(**LUIS** enters and mentally prepares himself for what is to come. Then, he takes out his phone, readies the camera, and places it discreetly in his locker.)*

(A long beat.)

*(**DANNY** enters, carrying an athletic bag.)*

DANNY. Diamonds! You just couldn't stay off the field for bye week, huh? Had to get a little extra training session with the ol QB? I see you! You told all those little Jessica Simpsons you had no time for Cabo!

LUIS. Yeah, uh. Look Danny. I don't want you gettin too excited. I just needed to get you down here.

DANNY. Straight to business? Okay, that's fine too.

LUIS. Yeah, straight to business.

(A beat.)

DANNY. So, you gonna put on some cleats?

LUIS. Danny, there's somethin I need to talk to you about. Somethin big.

DANNY. I'm starting to think you didn't call me down here to run that play action screen.

LUIS. You remember when you asked me, my first day here, what makes me tick?

DANNY. Yeah, and I remember you couldn't hardly tell me a damn thing.

LUIS. Maybe that's cuz I really didn't know. Maybe it was always too easy to say ain't nothin I'm chasin but that money, and be done with it.

DANNY. So you're telling me that you see now, now that we're really *doing this*, together, you see the importance of chasing greatness. Of building a legacy.

LUIS. Yeah. Yeah, I do see that now. I also see that greatness by itself ain't no different than money by itself. And legacy's bigger than Super Bowl wins. You thought about that before? Your legacy outside stats and rings?

DANNY. You want my honest answer to that? No. I haven't. Because the field is all that ever made sense to me. Dissecting coverage, going through my reads, putting the ball where my man's gonna be open. I step out there, and my world runs like clockwork. Because this is what I'm made to do. Every win, every accolade, is a testament to the fact that I found my one true calling. And I pursued it with no hesitation, no half-stepping / no...

LUIS. No thought to anything else?

DANNY. Exactly. I filtered out every distraction, every imaginable obstacle between myself and the title of greatest ever, and I kept my eyes on the prize.

LUIS. But what the fuck is the prize, Danny? A gold jacket? A big fuckin party? A ninety-nine rating in Madden? That's worth cuttin yourself off from everything else around you?

DANNY. Moreno, what the hell is this about?

LUIS. This is about somethin bigger than all the petty shit you and I been chasing our whole careers. This is about makin history. But you gotta see past the field if you gonna be a part of it. You gotta see past the end zones, past the stands and the fans and the banners and the blimps. Can you do that, Danny? Can you do that?

DANNY. You got ten seconds to say what you brought me here to say before I walk out that door.

LUIS. I'm not playin. Sunday after next. I'm not playin, Zeke ain't playin, shit, could be the whole defense ain't playin. We gonna show everybody across the fuckin country that it ain't no favor the owners are doin us by hiring us, it ain't no favor the coaches doin us puttin us on the field, it ain't no favor the fans doin us buyin tickets and jerseys and whatever, it's a favor we doin all these mothafuckas by steppin out on that field and puttin our bodies on the line. WE the ones who make the league and it's about damn time that we the ones who make the decisions. And if our coaches and the owners and the commissioner his damn self ain't gonna stand up for our rights, if they'd rather brown nose the racist bitch who apparently is boutta be the fuckin President, they don't get no games.

DANNY. Are you serious right now?

LUIS. I called you here cuz I want you to walk out with us. Right before the game. During the Anthem. Right out the stadium.

    *(A beat. **DANNY** is momentarily speechless.)*

We need you with us on this, Danny. Not just as our QB, but as our brother.

    *(**DANNY** breaks into a full-bodied laugh.)*

DANNY. So you're asking me to throw away my career, along with yours, along with all the work we've done all season? For...for what? To show the world I'm "woke" and that I *care*? Are you fucking concussed?

LUIS. Danny you gotta reel yourself in real quick and hear me out. I made my choice. Zeke made his. Now you can either step out on that field without us and get embarrassed, or walk out with us with that head held high.

DANNY. Fuck you Moreno! Not only am I gonna go out there and win, with or without you, but when Coach finds out about this you won't even be on the team for another week – you'll be out on your ass by fucking Friday, you hear me?

> *(A beat.)*
>
> *(**LUIS** approaches **DANNY** and gets in his face. This is calculated.)*
>
> *(Then, almost whispering into **DANNY**'s ear.)*

LUIS. So you're gonna go run to Daddy then, you little crybaby faggot?

> *(**DANNY** snaps. He punches **LUIS** in the face. Maybe he punches him again. Or even a third time.)*
>
> *(**DANNY** seethes. **LUIS** recovers. Then, **LUIS** grabs his phone from his locker. He shows **DANNY** that it has been recording the whole time.)*

Ain't a good look to have a suspendable offense caught on camera, week and a half before the biggest game of the season.

DANNY. Wha – you son of a bitch. You're going to fucking blackmail me? You think you can force me to join your harebrained fucking walk out by blackmailing me?

LUIS. No, I ain't forcin you to do nothin. But lemme tell you somethin you not doin: you not sayin shit to Coach about this. You ain't sayin shit to *nobody*. Unless you cool with this shit goin public on your bitch ass.

> *(**DANNY** snatches for Luis's phone; **LUIS** pulls it back.)*

You know you can't catch me, fool. I'm one step ahead. And when the books get written bout this era in the

league, it's gon be Kaep's face and mine on the cover
and you gon be a fuckin asterisk on a fuckin footnote.

(*A beat.*)

(**LUIS** *exits. Lights out.*)

Scene Fifteen

(Divisional Round Pregame: Mid-January.)

(The roar of a stadium full of ravenous fans echoes through the walls of the locker room. They've been with the team all season, and this is the moment they've all been waiting for. Playoffs...)

(Lights up on the locker room: **LUIS** *and* **EZEKIEL** *are fully suited.* **CRE'VON** *enters, also suited.)*

EZEKIEL. Creole, you made a decision yet?

CRE'VON. Nah Zeke, not yet. First I gotta talk to my man Luis for a second.

LUIS. Sup Creole.

CRE'VON. You remember, a few weeks back, when I told you that you my family?

> *(A beat.)*

From the time I was playin pee wee, my team always been my family. My truest family. My brothas. Not gon lie, it start to feel a lil different in college, ballin with niggas other than my homies from the hood. But this game forges bonds. It always has in my life. And here, witchyall, I feel like we been building somethin special.

LUIS. So whatchu sayin, Creole? You gon be with us?

CRE'VON. First I needa know: is it true? That you got some video you holdin over Danny's head?

> *(A beat.)*

I can't believe you really got me in here defending this white boy. I can't believe it. You called the dude a f...

you know what you said…knowin full well he'd snap, all so you could keep him from blabbin to Coach? Nigga why you do all that complicated shit when you shoulda never said a damn word to the man about this in the first place?

LUIS. Maybe I wanted to give him a chance, a chance to prove he's actually a bigger man than I thought he was. Then when he was boutta stab me in the back, I did what I had to do.

CRE'VON. I can't believe you really pulled this shit twice on me, dawg. I tell you some shit, on the down low, hopin it helps your ass fuckin step in somebody else shoes, and both times – both fuckin times – you take it and use that shit like as ammo in some fight.

> (**LUIS** *shrugs off this criticism.*)

Why you goin all street on folks that's supposed to be on the same side as you?

LUIS. It's just funny, Creole. It's this lil thing I learned from one of my teammates. He once told me the secret to winnin is to see what gets under your opponent's skin, then throw that shit their way. And eventually they crack. Make mistakes.

> (*A beat.* **CRE'VON** *realizes his own words are being used against him.*)

CRE'VON. Yeah, that's what you supposed to do to the other guy. Not the guy in the same suit as you.

LUIS. Maybe who the "other guy" is ain't about what colors he wearin anymore.

CRE'VON. Zeke, you agree with this right now? You okay with this?

> (**LUIS** *and* **CRE'VON** *both look to* **EZEKIEL**. *A pause…*)

EZEKIEL. There's a line in the sand now, Creole. I may not like how it went down, but Danny had a chance to step over. He made his decision.

CRE'VON. Huh. Well then. I'm out too.

> (**CRE'VON** *goes to leave, muttering as he exits.*)

(Under his breath.) Getting my damn agent to get me a goddamn trade to somewhere with less fuckin drama...

> (**LUIS** *and* **EZEKIEL** *decompress from the confrontation.*)

> (*Sounds of an* **ANNOUNCER** *("Aaaand now...") begin, as crowd noise dies down.* **LUIS** *and* **EZEKIEL** *regard one another.*)

LUIS. Let's make this happen, Zeke.

> (**EZEKIEL** *daps up* **LUIS** *and the two head out of the locker room.*)

> (*Lights out on the locker room as lights come up on the field, where* **CRE'VON** *and* **DANNY** *are already lined up side-by-side.*)

> (**LUIS** *and* **EZEKIEL** *join* **DANNY** *and* **CRE'VON** *as crowd noise intensifies.*)

> (*Tension brews in silence between the four men as the babbling of* **ANNOUNCERS** *blends with the cheers of fans. Maybe the voices become distorted. This moment stretches out like an exceptionally long period of discordant jazz (think Kamasi Washington), with a resolution seemingly lying somewhere far out of sight...then, all comes into focus.*)

ANNOUNCER #2.   And now, ladies and gentlemen, to honor America, please stand and remove your hats for tonight's performance of the national anthem!

> *(This moment should be aesthetically similar to Scene Five. But this time, **LUIS** and **EZEKIEL** both take a knee when the national anthem begins. Then, part of the way through the playing of the anthem, the music cuts out and is replaced by something like "Uncle Sam Goddamn" by Brother Ali* (while this song is exceptionally perfect for this moment – and part of the song even mentions the national anthem – another hip-hop protest song could work as well). **LUIS** and **EZEKIEL** stand up and walk out of the stadium. Maybe they walk through audience aisles. **CRE'VON** and **DANNY** are left onstage, frozen. The team is no more.)*

> *(Lights out.)*

---

* A licence to produce *Moreno* does not include a performance license for any third-party or copyrighted music. Licensees should create an original composition or use music in the public domain. For further information, please see the Music and Third Party Materials Use Note on page iii.

Scene Sixteen

(Divisional Round – Postgame. Conspicuous silence from the stadium crowd. **CRE'VON** *sits alone in the locker room, still in his gear, holding his helmet.)*

*(**DANNY** enters, also still in full gear, holding his helmet;* **CRE'VON** *drops his head.* **DANNY** *walks straight to his locker, heated.* **DANNY** *bursts out in anger: maybe he throws his helmet; maybe he slams his locker. But then, he composes himself. He starts putting his gear in his locker; he removes his shoulder pads and jersey and hangs them up.)*

*(**DANNY** then notices that* **CRE'VON**, *still sitting in full gear, has hardly moved.)*

DANNY. *(Sympathetically.)* Not your best game, huh?

(A beat.)

Hey, Cre'von. You left it all on the field.

CRE'VON. Did I? It barely even felt like I was out there. Ain't ever been so scrambled in my head, like I was steppin and my legs went the opposite way I thought they would.

DANNY. You weren't set up for success tonight. We weren't set up for success.

CRE'VON. Yeah, well. You still did ya part, Mr. 500 yards.

DANNY. No. No, I didn't. A loss is a fucking loss. And it went down like that because... I couldn't keep this team together.

CRE'VON. Ay, you don't gotta put that / on yourself

DANNY. Except that I do. I'm the leader of this team. And I let it fall apart when it mattered most.

CRE'VON. Seem we got pulled apart from a lotta angles.

DANNY. Yeah. Well.

> (**DANNY** *takes Cre'von's helmet, sets it in Cre'von's locker.*)

There's always next year.

CRE'VON. *(Unconvinced.)* Hm. You right. Always, always gon be next year.

> (*A beat.* **CRE'VON** *begins to see the whirlwind. Then, he snaps out of it, gets up, heads to his locker and begins to remove his gear.*)
>
> (*Lights out.*)

Scene Seventeen

(Lights up. **LUIS** *and* **EZEKIEL**, *outside the locker room, off the field, away from the cameras, are sitting together, smoking a joint. The mood is somber, but not desperate or hopeless.* **LUIS** *hits the joint and starts coughing incessantly. When he's finished.)*

LUIS. Shit you know I ain't hit that loud in a minute and a half.

EZEKIEL. Yeah well, can't really be doing that when you're on contract. They'd let you hit your fucking wife before they let you hit a joint.

LUIS. That's some real fucked shit. Think it's ever gon change?

EZEKIEL. The league-caring-too-much-about-weed part or the league-caring-not-enough-about-domestic-violence part?

LUIS. Fuck man, both. All of it. The whole-ass thing. The league caring about us part.

EZEKIEL. Shiiid, I ain't holding my breath.

*(**LUIS** takes a puff on the joint, starts conspicuously holding his breath. He keeps holding until he coughs again.)*

LUIS. Ay go check, go check if it's all better now.

*(**ZEKE** and **LUIS** share a laugh.)*

(A beat.)

I can't believe the other guys on defense didn't follow through. I really thought we convinced em.

EZEKIEL. Man as we were walking past Darnell I swear I saw that man in his eyes, tryna swim up from that sunken place.

LUIS. Whatchu sayin?

EZEKIEL. Man you haven't seen *Get Out*?

LUIS. Nah horror ain't really my thing.

EZEKIEL. Well, I felt like the real Darnell was trapped somewhere underneath, but the Darnell we saw was just...frozen in place. Unable to move.

LUIS. Shit, that's heavy. I can relate.

(*A beat.*)

EZEKIEL. I know how ingrained it must be, the instinct to keep close track of everybody's soft spots, to make sure you've always got something to give you the upper hand when push comes to shove. I'm sure tht kind of ruthlessness served you at some point in your life, but it's only ever a way to lift yourself. To lift up everyone... I don't know. We'll have to get more creative than that.

(*A beat.*)

So, what's your plan now?

LUIS. Well, I still think I got a chance to get signed somewhere else. I mean I don't got an agent no more, but... Ain't like all them owners meetin up in some racist Illuminati cave, schemin against us. There gotta be somebody willing to step outta line for me.

EZEKIEL. What if they are in a racist Illuminati cave, scheming against us?

LUIS. Then you know what, I don't wanna have shit to do with em. I got my money, and I'm out.

(**EZEKIEL** *smiles and takes from his pocket a couple bullet-shots of some dark liquor, passing one to* **LUIS**.)

EZEKIEL. To new beginnings.

(They clink and drink.)

(Lights out.)

End of Play

Lightning Source UK Ltd.
Milton Keynes UK
UKHW031253180322
400278UK00013B/153